Contents

Contents

Introduction

We came to Manderley in early May, arriving, so Maxim said, with the birds and the flowers before the start of summer. I can see myself now, badly dressed as usual, although I had been married for seven weeks. I wondered if he guessed that I feared my arrival at Manderley now as much as I had looked forward to it before.

Maxim de Winter is the owner of Manderley, a country house built of grey stone on the wild, dangerous coast of Cornwall, in south-west England. His clever, beautiful first wife Rebecca has died there, and Maxim goes to Monte Carlo to escape from the past. There he meets an ordinary young Englishwoman with very little experience of the world who works as a companion to a wealthy but difficult American woman.

The young woman is immediately attracted to Maxim and they marry. They spend a few happy weeks in Monte Carlo before Maxim takes her back to England. But her problems begin as soon as they arrive at Manderley.

They are met by the frightening housekeeper, Mrs Danvers, who clearly dislikes the new Mrs de Winter. Although it is more than a year since Rebecca died, her presence at Manderley remains very strong. Frank Crawley, Maxim's business manager, tells the new Mrs de Winter that Rebecca was 'the most beautiful creature I ever saw in my life'.

The more the new wife learns of Rebecca, the more she feels she cannot take her place. She feels that she lacks beauty, brains and confidence. She watches her husband grow cold towards her. She is at psychological war with Mrs Danvers. And she begins to wonder if she was wise to come to Manderley.

Rebecca is Daphne du Maurier's best-known and most popular book. Its opening line, 'Last night I dreamed I went to Manderley again', is one of the most famous first lines in English literature. The story has been translated into more than twenty languages and in 1940 it was first made into a film by British director Alfred Hitchcock. *Rebecca* was Hitchcock's first Hollywood film and he received a Best Picture Oscar for it. The film starred the famous English actors Laurence Olivier as Maxim and Joan Fontaine as the new Mrs de Winter. The story has been filmed for television several times since then.

Rebecca is a dark detective story with romantic and psychological tension, and we do not know how the story is going to end until the last paragraph. Readers particularly enjoy the character of the second Mrs de Winter. We never learn her name because she tells the story in the first person, but we watch her as she changes from an innocent and inexperienced young woman into a strong, loyal wife. She is wonderfully contrasted with the evil Mrs Danvers, who is always in the background as a threatening presence. We are sure nothing good can happen while Mrs Danvers is in the house. The new wife is also strongly contrasted with Rebecca, whose true character is gradually shown through the story. Rebecca's charming public face hid a very different person. Favell, Rebecca's cousin, is a smaller and meaner model of her, and he represents her in the story.

Daphne du Maurier was born on 13 May 1907 into 'a world of imagination,' as she once wrote. Her father, Gerald du Maurier, was the leading actor and manager at Wyndham's Theatre in London. Wyndham's, in Charing Cross Road, is still a theatre today. Daphne's mother acted too, and her grandfather was an artist and writer, so Daphne and her two sisters grew up in a world of literature and theatre. 'I suppose I was born into a world of . . . imagination,' she said later. 'I was always pretending to be someone else.' Daphne was educated at home until she was eighteen, when she went to France for six months. She read widely in English and French. She wrote short stories all through her teenage years.

In 1926 Daphne made a journey with her mother and sisters to Fowey in Cornwall. It changed her life. She fell in love with Cornwall and its people, and found ideas for her first full-length novel, *The Loving Spirit*. A young army officer called Frederick Browning read this romantic story and was deeply affected by it. Frederick sailed to Fowey in his boat to find the person who had written it. Clearly, he was romantic too. He found Daphne, fell in love with her and they married in 1932.

They spent most of their married life in Cornwall, where they had two daughters and one son. Du Maurier loved the West Country and her most popular books are set there. She died in Cornwall in 1989, aged 81. After her death, her ashes were taken to the Cornish cliffs that she loved.

Du Maurier wrote two main types of books. Her works of historical fiction are set in seventeenth and eighteenth-century Cornwall. These are romantic stories of adventure, violence and love. They show a strong feeling for the past, but also a sense of how our present lives are affected by past events. The most famous of these novels is *Jamaica Inn* (also a Penguin Reader), which came out in 1936, two years before *Rebecca*. It made the real Jamaica Inn – a pub with its own ghosts – into a popular tourist attraction. Other novels of this type include *Frenchman's Creek* (1941), *Hungry Hill* (1943) and *The King's General* (1946).

Du Maurier also wrote modern mystery novels, and these include *Rebecca* (1938), *My Cousin Rachel* (1951) and *The Scapegoat* (1957). In addition, she wrote many short stories. Two of these stories, 'The Birds' and 'Don't Look Now', were later made into famous Hollywood films. She also wrote non-fiction, including a book about her father's life, the story of her own life, books about Cornwall, and a study of Branwell Brontë (the brother of the writer Charlotte Brontë). Du Maurier was a great admirer of the Brontë family, and there are clear parallels between *Rebecca* and Charlotte Brontë's famous novel *Jane Eyre*. In both stories, a young woman falls in love with an older man. In each case, mystery surrounds the man's first wife. And in both stories the man's much-loved home is destroyed.

Rebecca is set in 1938, at the time when Du Maurier was writing the book. There is no reference to actual events happening then, particularly the approach of war in Europe, but it describes in detail the way of life in that period. Maxim de Winter is from a rich family with a country home – Manderley – and has a housekeeper, a business manager and servants, as many wealthy people did at that time. He has a car and a telephone, which only rich people were then able to afford. The characters behave towards each other in a formal way, according to their place in society. When Rebecca's cousin Favell is too friendly to Mrs de Winter, for example, she is shocked and not quite sure how to deal with the situation.

Society was very carefully ordered in those days. Everyone knew their place and most people accepted it. If you were born the child of a servant, you would probably be a servant yourself. The oldest son in an important family, like Maxim de Winter, was given the family home when his father died. Beatrice, Maxim's sister, has married and gone to live somewhere else.

Daphne du Maurier combined her experiences of two great houses to create the de Winter home, Manderley. As a child she stayed in an enormous country house in the north of England, where there were many servants and a very powerful housekeeper. There she learned how a country house could be run. When the Du Maurier family moved to Fowey, young Daphne spent a lot of time exploring. One day, she found Menabilly House, about thirty-five kilometres away. The house was hidden at the end of a long driveway. It was empty and forgotten, but Daphne loved it. Walking down from the house, she came to two beaches in a small bay. Beside one of the beaches was a little cottage. This provided the perfect setting for the story of Rebecca at Manderley.

Later Du Maurier moved to Menabilly House, and lived there for twenty-four years. Her love of nature is shown by the many descriptions of the gardens, the sea and the Cornish countryside in *Rebecca*. The natural world continues, whatever her characters are doing. 'Here at Manderley a new day was starting; the creatures in the garden were not concerned with our troubles,' says the second Mrs de Winter, perhaps envious of the blackbirds' freedom.

Chapter 1 Maxim de Winter

Last night I dreamed I went to Manderley again. It seemed to me that I was passing through the iron gates that led to the driveway. The drive was just a narrow track now, its stony surface covered with grass and weeds. Sometimes, when I thought I had lost it, it would appear again, beneath a fallen tree or beyond a muddy pool formed by the winter rains. The trees had thrown out new low branches which stretched across my way. I came to the house suddenly, and stood there with my heart beating fast and tears filling my eyes.

There was Manderley, our Manderley, secret and silent as it had always been, the grey stone shining in the moonlight of my dream. Time could not spoil the beauty of those walls, nor of the place itself, as it lay like a jewel in the hollow of a hand. The grass sloped down towards the sea, which was a sheet of silver lying calm under the moon, like a lake undisturbed by wind or storm. I turned again to the house, and I saw that the garden had run wild, just as the woods had done. Weeds were everywhere. But moonlight can play strange tricks with the imagination, even with a dreamer's imagination. As I stood there, I could swear that the house was not an empty shell, but lived and breathed as it had lived before. Light came from the windows, the curtains blew softly in the night air, and there, in the library, the door stood half open as we had left it, with my handkerchief on the table beside the bowl of autumn flowers.

Then a cloud came over the moon, like a dark hand across a face. The memories left me. I looked again at an empty shell, with no whisper of the past about its staring walls. Our fear and suffering were gone now. When I thought about Manderley in my waking hours I would not be bitter; I would think of it as it might have been, if I could have lived there without fear. I would remember the rose garden in summer, and the birds that sang there; tea under the trees, and the sound of the sea coming up to us from the shore below. I would think of the flowers blown from the bushes, and the Happy Valley. These things could never lose their freshness. They were memories that could not hurt. All this I knew in my dream (because, like most sleepers, I knew that I dreamed). In reality, I lay far away, in a foreign land, and would wake before long in my lonely little hotel bedroom. I would lie for a moment, stretch myself and turn, confused by that burning sun, that hard, clean sky, so different from the soft moonlight of my dream. The day would lie before us both, long no doubt, but full of a certain peace, a calm we had not known before. We would not talk of Manderley; I would not tell my dream. For Manderley was ours no longer. Manderley was no more.

We can never go back again; that is certain. The past is still too close to us. But we have no secrets from each other now; everything is shared. Our little hotel may be dull, and the food not very good; day after day, things may be very much the same. But dullness is better than fear. We live now very much by habit. And I have become very good at reading out loud. The only time I have known him show impatience is when the postman is delayed and we have to wait for our post from England. I have lost my old self-consciousness. I am very different from that person who drove to Manderley for the first time, hopeful and eager, filled with the desire to please. It was my lack of confidence, of course, that struck people like Mrs Danvers. What must I have seemed like, after Rebecca?

I can see myself now, so long ago, with my short straight hair and young, unpowdered face, dressed in a badly fitting coat and skirt, following Mrs Van Hopper into the hotel for lunch. She would go to her usual table in the corner, near the window, and, looking to left and right, would say, 'Not a single well-known face! I shall tell the manager he must make a reduction in my bill. What does he think I come here for? To look at the waiters?'

We ate in silence, as Mrs Van Hopper liked to think about nothing but her food. Then I saw that the table next to ours, which had been empty for three days, was to be used once more. The head waiter was showing the new arrival to his place. Mrs Van Hopper put down her fork and stared. Then she leaned over the table to me, her small eyes bright with excitement, her voice a little too loud.

'It's Max de Winter,' she said, 'the man who owns Manderley. You've heard of it, of course. He looks ill, doesn't he? They say he hasn't been the same since his wife's death. The papers were full of it, of course. They say he never talks about it, never mentions her name. She was drowned, you know, in the bay near Manderley . . .'

Her interest in other people was like a disease. I can see her as though it were yesterday, on that unforgettable afternoon, wondering how to make her attack. Suddenly, she turned to me. 'Go upstairs quickly and find that letter from my brother's son, the one with the photograph. Bring it down to me immediately.'

I saw then that she had made her plan. I wished I had the courage to warn the stranger. But when I returned, I saw that she had not waited; he was already sitting beside her. I gave her the letter, without a word. He rose to his feet immediately.

'Mr de Winter is having coffee with us; go and ask the waiter for another cup,' she said, just carelessly enough to warn him what I was. Her expression showed that I was young and unimportant, and that there was no need to include me in the conversation. So it was a surprise when he remained standing and made a sign to the waiter.

'I'm afraid I must disagree,' he said to her. 'You are both having coffee with me,' and before I knew what had happened he was sitting on my usual chair and I was beside Mrs Van Hopper.

3

For a moment she looked annoyed. Then she leaned forward, holding the letter.

'You know, I recognized you as soon as you walked in,' she said, 'and I thought, "Why, there's Mr de Winter, Billy's friend; I simply *must* show him the photographs of Billy and his wife." And here they are, bathing at Palm Beach. Billy is mad about her. He hadn't met her, of course, when he gave that party where I saw you first. But I don't expect you remember an old woman like me?'

'Yes, I remember you very well,' he said. 'I don't think I should care for Palm Beach. That sort of thing has never amused me.'

Mrs Van Hopper gave her fat laugh. 'If Billy had a home like Manderley, he wouldn't want to play around in Palm Beach,' she said. She paused, expecting him to smile, but he went on smoking, looking just a little disturbed.

'I've seen pictures of it, of course,' she said, 'and it looks perfectly beautiful. I remember Billy telling me it was lovelier than any other house of its size and age. I am surprised you can ever bear to leave it.'

His silence was painful, as anyone else would have noticed, but she continued, 'You Englishmen are all the same about your homes,' her voice becoming louder, 'you don't want to seem proud of them. Isn't there a great hall at Manderley, with some very valuable pictures?'

I think he realized my discomfort; he leaned forward in his chair and spoke to me, his voice gentle, asking if I would have some more coffee, and when I shook my head I felt that his eyes were still resting on me, wondering.

'What brings you here?' Mrs Van Hopper went on. 'You're not one of the regular visitors. What are your plans?'

'I haven't made up my mind,' he said, 'I came away in rather a hurry.'

His own words must have raised a memory, for he looked disturbed again. She talked on, still not noticing. 'Of course you miss Manderley. The West Country must be lovely in the spring.'

'Yes,' he said shortly. 'Manderley was looking its best.'

In the end it was a waiter who gave him his opportunity, with a message for Mrs Van Hopper. He got up immediately, pushing back his chair. 'Don't let me keep you,' he said.

'It's so nice to have met you like this, Mr de Winter; I hope I shall see something of you. You must come and have a drink some time. I have one or two people coming in tomorrow evening. Why not join us?' I turned away so that I did not have to watch him search for an excuse.

'I'm so sorry,' he said, 'tomorrow I am probably driving to Sospel; I'm not sure when I shall get back.'

Looking a little annoyed, she left it, and he went.

◆

The next morning Mrs Van Hopper woke with a sore throat and a rather high temperature. Her doctor told her to stay in bed. I left her quite happy, after the arrival of a nurse, and went down early for lunch – a good half-hour before our usual time. I expected the room to be empty, and it was – except for the table next to ours. I was not prepared for this. I thought he had gone to Sospel. I was halfway across the room before I saw him, and could not go back. This was a situation for which I was not trained. I wished I was older, different. I went to our table, looking straight ahead. But as soon as I sat down, I knocked over the bowl of flowers. The water ran over the cloth, and down onto my legs. The waiter was at the other end of the room and did not see. In a second, though, my neighbour was at my side.

'You can't sit with a wet tablecloth,' he said, 'you won't enjoy your food. Get out of the way.' He began to dry the table with his handkerchief, and then the waiter came hurrying to help.

'Lay my table for two,' he said. 'This lady will have lunch with me.'

'Oh, no,' I said, 'I couldn't possibly.'

'Why not?'

I tried to think of an excuse. I knew he did not want to lunch with me. He was only being polite.

'Come and sit down. We needn't talk unless we want to.'

He sat down, and went on eating his lunch as though nothing had happened. I knew we could go on like this, all through the meal, without speaking but without any sense of awkwardness.

'Your friend,' he began at last, 'she is very much older than you. Have you known her long?'

'She's not really a friend,' I told him, 'she is an employer. She's training me to be a companion, and she pays me.'

'I did not know one could buy companionship,' he said; 'it sounds a strange idea. You haven't much in common with her. What do you do it for? Haven't you any family?'

'No – they're dead.'

'You know,' he said, 'we've got that in common, you and I. We are both alone in the world. Oh, I've got a sister, though we don't see much of each other, and an ancient grandmother whom I visit two or three times a year, but neither of them provides much companionship. You know, I think you've made a big mistake in coming here, in joining forces with Mrs Van Hopper. You're not made for that sort of job. You're too young, for one thing, and too soft. Now go upstairs and put your hat on, and I'll have the car brought round.'

I was happy that afternoon; I can remember it well. I can see the blue sky and sea. I can feel again the wind on my face, and hear my laugh, and his that answered it. It was not the Monte Carlo that I had known before. The harbour was a dancing thing, bright with boats, and the sailors were cheerful, smiling men, careless as the wind. I can remember as though I were still wearing it my comfortable, badly fitting suit, my broad hat, the shoes I wore. I had never looked more youthful; I had never felt so old.

I am glad it cannot happen twice, the fever of first love. For it is a fever, and a misery too, whatever the poets may say. One is so easily hurt.

I have forgotten much of Monte Carlo, of those morning drives, of where we went, even of our conversation; but I have not forgotten how my fingers trembled, pulling on my hat, and how I would run down the stairs and go outside. He would be there, in the driver's seat, reading a paper while he waited, and when he saw me he would smile, and throw it behind him into the back seat, and open the door, saying, 'Well, how is the companion this morning, and where does she want to go?' If he had driven round in circles it would not have mattered to me.

Chapter 2 Manderley

We came to Manderley in early May, arriving, so Maxim said, with the birds and the flowers before the start of summer. I can see myself now, badly dressed as usual, although I had been married for seven weeks. I wondered if he guessed that I feared my arrival at Manderley now as much as I had looked forward to it before. Gone was my excitement, my happy pride. I was like a child brought to her first school. Any confidence I had gained during my seven weeks of marriage was gone now.

'You mustn't mind if there's a certain amount of interest in you,' he said. 'Everyone will want to know what you are like. They have probably talked of nothing else for weeks. You've only got to be yourself and they will all love you. And you won't have to worry about the house; Mrs Danvers does everything. Just leave it all to her. She'll be stiff with you at first, I expect. She's an unusual character, but you mustn't let her worry you.'

We drove through two high iron gates and up the long driveway. We stopped at the wide stone steps at the open door, and two servants came down to meet us.

'Well, here we are, Frith,' said Maxim to the older one, taking off his hat. 'And this is Robert,' he added, turning towards me. We walked together up the steps, Frith and Robert following with my coat and travelling bag.

'This is Mrs Danvers,' said Maxim.

Someone came forward from the sea of faces, someone tall and thin, dressed in black, with great dark eyes in a white face. When she took my hand, hers was heavy and deathly cold and it lay in mine like a lifeless thing. Her eyes never left mine. I cannot remember her words now, but I know she welcomed me to Manderley, in a stiff little speech spoken in a voice as cold and lifeless as her hand had been. When she had finished, she waited, as though for a reply, and I tried to say something, dropping my hat in my confusion. She bent to pick it up, and as she handed it to me I saw a little smile of scorn on her lips.

After tea Frith came in. 'Mrs Danvers wondered, madam, whether you would like to see your room.'

Maxim looked up. 'How did they get on with the east wing?' he said.

'Very well, sir. Mrs Danvers was rather afraid it would not be finished by your return. But the men left last Monday. I think you will be very comfortable, sir; it's a lot lighter, of course, on that side of the house.'

'What have they been doing?' I asked.

'Oh, nothing much. Only redecorating and changing the furniture in the rooms in the east wing, which I thought we would use for ours. As Frith says, it's much more cheerful on that side of the house, and it has a lovely view of the rose garden. It was the visitors' wing when my mother was alive. I'll just finish reading these letters and then I'll come up and join you. Run along and make friends with Mrs Danvers. It's a good opportunity.'

The black figure stood waiting for me at the top of the stairs, her dark eyes watching me from her pale face. We went along broad passages, then came to a door which she opened, standing back to let me pass. There was a large double bedroom with wide windows, and a bathroom on the far side. I went straight to the windows. The rose garden lay below, and, beyond it, a smooth grass bank stretching to the woods.

'You can't see the sea from here, then,' I said, turning to Mrs Danvers.

'No, not from this wing,' she answered, 'you can't even hear it. You would not know the sea was anywhere near, from this wing.'

She spoke in a strange way, as though something lay behind her words – as though there was something wrong with this wing.

'I'm sorry about that; I like the sea.'

She did not answer; she just went on looking at me, her hands folded in front of her.

'But it's a very beautiful room, and I'm sure we shall be very comfortable. I understand that it has been redecorated.'

'Yes.'

'What was it like before?'

'There was blue paper on the walls, and there were different curtains. Mr de Winter did not find it very cheerful. It was never used much, except for occasional visitors. But Mr de Winter gave special orders in his letter that you were to have this room.'

'Then this was not his bedroom originally?'

'No, madam; he's never used the rooms in this wing before.'

'Oh. He didn't tell me that.'

There was silence between us. I wished she would go away. I wondered why she had to go on standing there, watching me, her hands folded on her black dress.

'I suppose you have been at Manderley for many years,' I said, making another effort, 'longer than anyone else?'

'Not so long as Frith,' she said, and I thought again how lifeless her voice was, and how cold. 'Frith was here when the old gentleman was living, when Mr de Winter was a boy.'

'I see; so you did not come until after that.'

'No. Not until after that. I came here when Mr de Winter married his first wife,' she said, and her voice, which had been dull and flat, was suddenly filled with unexpected life, and there was a spot of colour in her bony face. The change was so sudden that I was disturbed. I did not know what to do or to say. It was as though she had spoken words which were forbidden, words which she had hidden within herself for a long time and now would be kept in no longer. I could see that she scorned me, seeing that I was no great lady, but was ordinary and awkward. Yet there was something beside scorn in those eyes of hers, something surely of positive dislike, or actual hatred?

I had to say something; I could not let her see how much I feared and mistrusted her.

'Mrs Danvers,' I heard myself saying, 'I hope we shall be friends and come to understand one another. You must have patience with me, you know, because this sort of life is new to me; I've lived rather differently. But I do want to make a success of it, and above all to make Mr de Winter happy. I know I can leave arrangements in the house to you, and you must just run things as they have always been run. I shan't want to make any changes.'

I stopped, rather breathless, and when I looked up again I saw that she had moved, and was standing with her hand on the handle of the door.

'Very good,' she said. 'I hope I shall do everything to your satisfaction. The house has been in my charge now for more than a year, and Mr de Winter has never complained. It was very different of course when the first Mrs de Winter was alive; there were many visitors then, a lot of parties, and though I managed things for her, she liked to give the orders herself.'

Once again I felt that she chose her words with care, and was watching for their effect on my face.

'I would rather leave it to you,' I repeated, 'much rather,' and into her face came the same expression I had noticed before, when I first shook hands with her in the hall, a look of scorn. I wished she would go; she was like a shadow standing there.

'If you find anything not to your liking, you will tell me immediately?'

'Yes,' I said, 'yes, of course, Mrs Danvers,' but I knew this was not what she had meant to say, and silence fell between us once again.

◆

'Dislike you? Why dislike you? What the devil do you mean?' He turned from the window, an angry look on his face. I wondered why he should mind, and wished I had said something else.

'I mean, it must be much easier for her to look after a man alone. I expect she had got used to doing it, and perhaps she was afraid I would be difficult.'

'Difficult, my God . . .' he began, 'if you think . . .' and then he stopped, and kissed me on the top of my head.

'Let's forget about Mrs Danvers,' he said. 'She doesn't interest me very much. Come along, and let me show you something of Manderley.'

Chapter 3 The Cottage in the Bay

I had never realized that life at Manderley would be so orderly and planned. I remember now, looking back, how on that first morning Maxim was up and dressed and writing letters even before breakfast, and how when I came downstairs I found he had nearly finished. He looked up at me and smiled.

'You mustn't mind,' he said, 'this is something you must get used to. Running a place like Manderley is hard work. By the way, my sister Beatrice has written to ask her husband Giles and herself over to lunch. I half expected she would. I suppose she wants to have a look at you.'

'Today?' I said, my heart sinking.

'Yes. She won't stay long. You'll like her, I think. She's very honest. If she doesn't like you, she'll tell you so to your face.'

I found this hardly comforting.

'I've a lot of things to deal with this morning. I must see Frank Crawley, who looks after my affairs. I've been away too long. He'll be in to lunch too, by the way.' Then he picked up his letters and went out of the room, and I remember thinking that this was not how I had imagined my first morning.

◆

After lunch Beatrice and I went out, and walked around slowly on the smooth green grass.

'I think it's a pity you came back to Manderley so soon,' said Beatrice, 'it would have been far better to travel in Italy for three or four months, and come back in the middle of the summer. It would have done Maxim good too, besides being easier for you. I can't help feeling that it's going to be rather difficult for you here at first.'

'Oh, I don't think so,' I said. 'I know I shall learn to love Manderley.'

She did not answer, and we walked up and down across the grass.

'Tell me a bit about yourself,' she said at last. 'What was it you were doing in the south of France? Living with some terrible American woman, Maxim said.'

I explained about Mrs Van Hopper, and what had led to it, and she seemed sympathetic but distant, as though she were thinking of something else.

'Yes,' she said. 'It all happened very suddenly. But of course we were all very pleased, my dear, and I do hope you will both be happy.'

I wondered why she said she hoped we would be happy, instead of saying she knew we would be so. She was kind, she was sincere, I liked her very much, but there was a shade of doubt in her voice that made me feel afraid.

'Poor Maxim,' she said, 'he went through a terrible time, and let's hope you have made him forget about it. We are not a bit like each other. I show everything on my face – whether I like people or not, whether I am angry or pleased. Maxim is completely different. Very quiet. You never know what's going on in that funny mind of his. I lose my temper easily, quarrel hard, and then it's all over. Maxim loses his temper once or twice in a year – and when he does, he really loses it. I don't suppose he ever will with you; I should think you are a calm little thing.'

She looked away from me, her hands in her pockets, and examined the house in front of us.

'You're not using the west wing, then?' she said.

'No. We are in the east wing. It has all been got ready specially.'

'Has it? I didn't know that. I wonder why.'

'It was Maxim's idea. He seems to prefer it.'

She said nothing, but went on looking at the windows. 'How do you get on with Mrs Danvers?' she asked suddenly.

'I haven't seen much of her. She frightens me a bit. I've never seen anyone quite like her before.'

'I don't suppose you have,' said Beatrice. 'There's no need to be frightened of her, and don't let her see it, whatever you do. Did she seem friendly?'

'No, not very.'

'I shouldn't have more to do with her than you can help. Of course she's madly jealous. I was afraid she would be.'

'Why? Why should she be jealous? Maxim doesn't seem to be particularly fond of her.'

'My dear child, it's not Maxim she's thinking of. No. She dislikes your being here at all – that's the trouble.'

'Why? Why should she dislike me?'

'I thought you knew. I thought Maxim would have told you. She loved Rebecca so much.'

'Oh,' I said. 'Oh, I see.'

When the Lacys were leaving, Beatrice took my hand, then, bending down, gave me a quick kiss. 'Goodbye,' she said. 'Forgive me if I've asked you a lot of rude questions, my dear, and said all sorts of things I shouldn't. Politeness never was my strong point, as Maxim will tell you. And you're not a bit what I expected.' She looked straight at me. 'You see,' she said, starting towards the door, 'you're so different from Rebecca.'

We watched the car disappear round the curve of the drive, and then Maxim took my arm and said, 'Thank goodness for that! Get a coat quickly, and come out – never mind the rain; I want a walk. I can't stand sitting around.'

He called to his dog, Jasper, and we headed towards the sea. We soon came to a place in the woods where there were two paths leading in different directions. The dog took the right-hand path.

'Not that way,' called Maxim, 'come on, Jasper, old boy!'

The dog looked back at us, but did not move.

'Why does he want to go that way?' I asked.

'I suppose he's used to it,' said Maxim. 'It leads to a little bay, where we used to keep a boat. Come on, boy! Jasper!'

We turned onto the left-hand path.

'This brings us to what we call the Happy Valley. There! Look at that.'

We stood on the slope of a wooded hill, and the path ran on

ahead of us into a valley, by the side of a running stream. On either side were flowering bushes, pink, white and gold, bending their heads in the summer rain. The air was full of their lovely smells. We wandered down into the valley. At the end of the path the flowers joined above our heads. We bent down to pass under them, and when I stood straight again, brushing the raindrops from my hair, I saw that we were standing in a little bay, the stones hard and white under our feet and the waves breaking on the shore beyond us. Maxim smiled down at me, watching my face.

'It's a surprise, isn't it?' he said. 'No one ever expects it. It's so sudden.'

We walked on the shore, playing with the dog and throwing stones into the sea. Then we looked round, and found that Jasper had disappeared. We called and whistled, but he did not come. Then, beyond the rocks to the right of the bay, I heard him.

'Hear that? He's over that way.' I began to climb over the slippery rocks.

'Come back!' said Maxim sharply. 'We don't want to go that way. The fool of a dog must look after himself. He knows his own way back.'

I pretended not to hear, and went on as best I could, climbing and slipping over the wet rocks. Then, looking up, I saw with surprise that I was in another bay. A stone wall had been built out from it to form a little harbour. Where the woods met the shore there was a long low building, half boathouse, half cottage, built of the same stone as the sea wall. There was a man on the beach, a fisherman perhaps, in long boots, and Jasper was running round and jumping at him. But the man took no notice; he was bending down, digging among the stones.

The man looked up at the sound of my footsteps.

'Good day,' he said. 'Dirty, isn't it?'

He had small eyes, a red, wet mouth and an empty foolish face. He watched me with interest, smiling all the time. 'Digging for

15

shells,' he said. 'No shells here. Been digging ever since the morning.'

'Oh,' I said. 'I'm sorry you can't find any.'

'That's right. No shells here.'

'Come on, Jasper,' I said, 'it's getting late. Come on, old boy!'

But Jasper was noisy and stupid, running round after nothing at all, excited perhaps by the wind and the sea. I saw that he would never follow me. I turned to the man, who had bent down again to his useless digging.

'Have you got any string?'

'Eh?'

'Have you got any string?'

'No shells here. Been digging since morning.' And he wiped his pale blue watery eyes.

'I want some string for the dog. He won't follow me.'

'Eh?' he said, and smiled his foolish smile.

'All right. It doesn't matter.'

I wondered if there was any string in the boathouse, and walked to it. To my surprise, the door was not locked, so I went inside, expecting to find the usual nets and boating equipment. But I was in a proper room, with tables, chairs and a bed pushed against the wall. There were bookshelves, with books in them, cups and plates, and on the shelves little model ships. But no one lived here. It was cold, and very dusty. I did not like it. I opened a door at the end of the room. Here were the ropes I had expected, a sail or two, paint pots, and on a shelf a ball of string and an old knife. They would do.

When I came out of the cottage, not looking behind me, the man was not digging any more; he was watching me, Jasper at his side. I bent down and this time Jasper allowed me to tie the string to his collar.

'I saw you go in there,' the man said, staring at me with his narrow watery eyes.

'Yes. It's all right. Mr de Winter won't mind.'

'She don't go in there now,' he said.

'No.'

'She's gone in the sea, hasn't she? She won't come back no more?'

'No. She'll not come back.'

'I never said nothing, did I?'

'No, of course not; don't worry.'

He bent down again to his digging, talking quietly to himself. I went across the stones and saw Maxim waiting for me by the rocks, his hands in his pockets.

'I'm sorry,' I said. 'Jasper wouldn't come. I had to get some string.'

He turned sharply, and started towards the woods.

'I'm sorry I was such a time. It was Jasper's fault. He kept running round the man. Who was he?'

'Only Ben. He's quite harmless, poor devil. His father was one of the farm servants. Where did you get that string?'

'I found it in the cottage.'

Maxim did not reply. He walked very fast, and the path was steep.

'Come on, Jasper! Make him walk faster, can't you? Pull that string.'

'It's your fault. You're walking so quickly. We can't keep up with you.'

'If you had listened to me instead of rushing off over those rocks, we would have been home by now. Jasper knew his way back. I can't think what you wanted to go after him for.'

'I thought he might have fallen and hurt himself. And I was afraid of the tide.'

'Is it likely that I would have left the dog if there had been any danger from the tide? I told you not to go on those rocks, and now you're complaining because you're tired.'

17

'Anyone would be tired, walking at this speed. I thought you'd come with me when I went after Jasper, instead of staying behind.'

'Why should I run after the miserable dog?'

'You just say that because you haven't got any other excuse.'

'Excuse for what?'

'Excuse for not coming with me over the rocks.'

'Well, and why do you think I didn't want to cross to the other bay?'

'Oh, Maxim – how should I know? I'm not a mind reader. I know you didn't want to, that's all. I could see it in your face.'

'See what in my face?'

'I've already told you. I could see that you didn't want to go.'

'All right – I didn't want to go to the other bay. Will that please you? I never go near the place, or that miserable cottage. And if you had my memories you would not want to go there either, or talk about it, or even *think* about it. There! I hope that satisfies you.'

His face was white, his eyes watering, with that dark, lost look they had had when I first met him. I put out my hand to his and held it tight.

'Please, Maxim, please!' I said.

'What's the matter?' he answered roughly.

'I don't want you to look like that. It hurts too much. Please, Maxim. Let's forget everything we said. A stupid, senseless argument. I'm sorry, dear. I'm sorry. Please let everything be all right.'

'We ought to have stayed in Italy,' he said. 'We ought never to have come back to Manderley. Oh God, what a fool I was to come back!'

Chapter 4 The Shadow of Rebecca

The next day I met Frank Crawley on the drive. He took off his hat and smiled. He seemed glad to see me. I smiled back at him. It was nice of him to be glad to see me. I liked Frank Crawley. I did not find him dull, as Beatrice did. Perhaps it was because I was dull myself. We walked along together.

'I was down in one of the bays the other day,' I said, 'the one with the little harbour. Jasper was behaving badly, running round that poor man who seems so foolish.'

'You must mean Ben. He's always on the shore. He's quite a nice person; you need never be frightened of him. He would not hurt a fly.'

'Oh, I wasn't frightened,' I said. I waited a moment, to gain confidence. 'I'm afraid that cottage place will be ruined,' I said lightly. 'I had to go in to find a bit of string to tie up Jasper. It's so cold and wet that the books are all getting spoilt. Why isn't something done about it? It seems such a pity.'

I knew he would not answer immediately. He bent down to tie up his shoe. 'I think if Maxim wanted anything done, he would tell me.'

'Are they all Rebecca's things?'

'Yes.'

'What did she use the cottage for? It looked quite lived-in. I thought from the outside it was just a boathouse.'

'It was a boathouse originally.' He sounded uncomfortable. 'Then – then she changed it . . . had furniture put in, and books.'

'Did she use it much?'

'Yes, she did. For moonlight swims and – and one thing and another.'

'What fun! Moonlight swimming must be lovely. Did you ever go?'

'Once or twice.'

I pretended not to notice how quiet he had become; he clearly did not want to speak about these things.

'What is the little harbour for?'

'The boat used to be kept there.'

'What boat?'

'Her boat.'

A strange sort of excitement was on me. I had to go on with my questions. He did not want to talk about it. I knew that. But I could not be silent.

'What happened to it? Was that the boat she was sailing when she was drowned?'

'Yes. It turned over and sank. She was washed overboard.'

'What sort of size was it?'

'Pretty small. It had a little place to sleep in.'

'What made it turn over?'

'It can be very windy in the bay.'

'Couldn't someone have got out to her?'

'Nobody saw the accident; nobody knew she had gone.'

'They *must* have known up at the house!'

'No. She often went out alone like that. She would come back at any time of night, and sleep at the cottage on the shore.'

'Did – did Maxim mind her going off alone like that?'

He waited a minute, and then shook his head. 'I don't know,' he said shortly. I felt he was being loyal to someone. Either to Maxim or to Rebecca, or perhaps even to himself. I did not know what to make of it.

'She must have been drowned, then, trying to swim to shore?'

'Yes.'

I imagined how the little boat would rock from side to side, and how the water would suddenly rush in and the sails push her down. It must have been very dark out there in the bay. The shore must have seemed very far away to anyone swimming there, in the water.

20

'How long afterwards did they find her?'

'About two months.'

Two months? I thought drowned people were found after about two days. I thought they would be washed up when the tide came in.

'Where did they find her?'

'Near Edgecoombe – about sixty kilometres up the coast.'

'How did they know it was her – after two months, how could they tell?' I wondered why he paused before each sentence, as though carefully considering his words. Had he cared for her, then; had he minded so much?

'Maxim went up to Edgecoombe to see the body. He recognized her.'

Suddenly I did not want to ask him any more. I felt sick. I hated myself. And there was an awkwardness between us that could not be ignored.

'Frank,' I said hopelessly, 'I know what you're thinking. You can't understand why I asked all those questions just now. You think that I'm interested in a – in a rather unpleasant way. It's not that. It's only that – that sometimes I feel myself at such a disadvantage. It's all strange to me, living here at Manderley. It's not the sort of life I'm used to. I know people are looking me up and down, wondering what I will make of it. I can imagine them saying 'What on earth does Maxim see in her?' And then, Frank, I begin to wonder myself, and I have a fearful feeling that I should never have married Maxim, that we are not going to be happy. I know that they are all thinking the same thing – "How different she is from Rebecca".'

I stopped, breathless, and already a little ashamed of myself.

Frank turned to me, looking very troubled. 'Mrs de Winter, please don't think that,' he said. 'I cannot tell you how glad I am that you have married Maxim. It will make all the difference to his life. I know you will make a great success of it. And if people round here make you feel that they are finding fault, it's – well – it's most terribly rude of them. I have never heard a word of it, though.'

'Thank you, Frank. What you say helps a lot. I expect I have been very stupid. I'm not good at meeting new people. I've never had to do it. And all the time I keep remembering how – how it must have been at Manderley before, when there was somebody here who was born to it, and did it all naturally and without effort. And I realize every day that she possessed the things I lack – confidence, beauty, brains – all the qualities that mean most in a woman. It doesn't help, Frank.'

He said nothing, but he went on looking anxious. 'You must not say that,' he said.

'Why not? It's true.'

'You have qualities that are just as important. Far more so, in fact. I don't know you very well. I'm not married, and I don't know much about women, but I would say that kindness, and honesty and – if I may say so – modesty, are worth far more to a husband than all the brains and beauty in the world.'

He looked worried still. 'I'm sure that Maxim would be very disturbed if he knew how you felt. I don't think he can have any idea of it. You are fresh and young and sensible; you have nothing to do with all that time that has gone. Forget it, Mrs de Winter, as he has done, thank heaven, and the rest of us. We none of us want to bring back the past. Maxim least of all. And it's for you, you know, to lead us away from it. Not to take us back there again.'

He was right, of course. Dear, good Frank. 'I ought to have told you this before. I feel happier – much happier. And I have you for my friend, whatever happens, haven't I, Frank?'

'Yes, of course.'

'Frank, before we put an end to this conversation, for ever, will you answer just one question?'

'Very well. I will do my best.'

'Tell me,' I said lightly, as though I did not care a bit, 'tell me, was Rebecca very beautiful?'

Frank waited a moment. I could not see his face; he was looking away from me, towards the house. 'Yes,' he said slowly, 'yes – I suppose she was the most beautiful creature I ever saw in my life.'

We went up the steps, into the hall, and I rang the bell for tea.

Chapter 5 Rebecca's Room

Maxim had to go up to London at the end of June to some public dinner. He was away for two days, and I was left alone. After lunch, I called Jasper, and we set off towards the shore. Jasper led the way, and went straight to the bay where the harbour was. The door of the cottage was not quite closed. I pushed it open and looked inside. Nothing had changed. Then I heard a noise in the boatstore.

'Is anybody there?' No answer. I looked round the edge of the door. Someone was trying to hide behind one of the sails. It was Ben.

'What's the matter? Do you want something?'

He looked at me stupidly, his mouth open.

'I'm not doing nothing,' he said.

'I think you'd better come out,' I said. 'Mr de Winter doesn't like people walking in and out of here.'

He got up, one hand behind his back.

'What have you got, Ben?' I asked. He obeyed like a child, showing me his hand. There was a fishing line in it. 'I'm not doing nothing,' he said again. 'I done nothing. I don't want to be put in the madhouse.' A tear rolled down his dirty face. 'You're not like the other one, though.'

'Who do you mean? What other one?'

'Tall and dark she was. She gave you the feeling of a snake. I've seen her here with my own eyes. By night, she'd come. I've seen her.' He paused, watching me closely. I did not say anything. 'I looked in on her once, and she shouted at me, she did. "You don't know me, do you?" she said. "You've never seen me here, and you won't again. If I catch you looking through the windows here I'll have you put in the madhouse. You wouldn't like that, would you? They're cruel to people in the madhouse." "I won't say nothing, madam," I said, and I touched my cap, like this. She's gone now, hasn't she?' he added anxiously.

'I don't know who you mean,' I said slowly; 'no one is going to put you in the madhouse. Good afternoon, Ben.'

I walked up the path. Poor thing – he was mad, of course. He didn't know what he was talking about. It was hardly likely that anyone would threaten him with the mental hospital. Maxim had said he was quite harmless, and so had Frank. Suddenly I wanted to run. I had been a fool to come to this bay. I should have gone to the other bay, by Happy Valley.

When I got back to the house there was no one about. It was too early for tea. But I had not been long in the sitting room when I heard a footstep, and a man came into the room. He did not see me at first, but when he did he looked quite surprised. I might have been the thief, and he the master of the house. He was a big, strong man, good-looking in a rather self-conscious, sunburnt way. He had the hot blue eyes of a heavy drinker. In a few years' time he would certainly be fat. His mouth was soft and pink, and he smelt of drink. He began to smile – the sort of smile he would give to every woman.

'I hope I didn't frighten you,' he said.

'No – of course not. I – I didn't expect visitors this afternoon.'

'What a shame – it's too bad of me to come in like this. The fact is, I came to see Mrs Danvers. She's an old friend of mine.'

'Oh, of course – it's quite all right.'

'How's old Max?'

I was surprised at his question. It sounded as though he knew him well. But it was strange to hear Maxim spoken of as Max. No one called him that.

'He's very well, thank you. He's gone up to London.'

'And left you all alone? That's too bad. Isn't he afraid someone will come and carry you off?'

He laughed. I did not like his laugh. I did not like him, either. Just then Mrs Danvers came into the room. She turned her eyes towards me, and I felt quite cold. How she seemed to hate me!

'Hullo, Danny. There you are! Aren't you going to introduce me?'

'This is Mr Favell, madam.' She spoke quietly, as if she would have preferred to say nothing at all.

'How do you do?' I said.

'Well, I suppose I'd better be going. Come out and have a look at my car.' He still spoke in a familiar and unpleasant way. I did not want to go and look at his car. I felt awkward, but could not think of an excuse.

'Where is it?'

'Round the corner; I didn't drive to the door – I was afraid of disturbing you. I had some idea you probably rested in the afternoon.'

I said nothing. The lie was too obvious. We walked out to his car, a green sports thing, typical of its owner.

'Come for a drive down to the gates?'

'No, I don't think I will. I'm rather tired.'

'You don't think it would look too good for the wife of the master of Manderley to be seen driving with someone like me, is that it?' he laughed.

'Oh, no,' I said, turning rather red. 'No, really.'

'Oh, well – goodbye. By the way, it would be very sporting of you not to say anything to Max about my little visit. He doesn't quite approve of me, I'm afraid, and it might get poor old Danny into trouble.'

'No,' I said awkwardly, 'all right.'

'Very sporting of you. Sure you won't change your mind and come for a drive? No? Goodbye, then.' The car shot down the drive.

I walked slowly back to the house. Maxim was away; I was supposed to be out on a long walk. It was Frith's day out, and the other servants were usually upstairs changing the beds during the afternoon. Favell had chosen his time well to call on Mrs Danvers. Too well. Who was he? As I stood in the hall the thought suddenly came to me that perhaps Mrs Danvers was dishonest, that she was doing something behind Maxim's back. Supposing this man Favell was a thief, and Mrs Danvers was in his pay? There were valuable things in the west wing. I suddenly decided to go upstairs and see for myself. My heart was beating in a strange, excited way.

Upstairs, there was no sound at all. I was uncertain which way to go. The plan of the rooms was not familiar to me. But I turned the handle of a door and went inside. It was dark; the curtains were closed. I turned the light on, and with a shock of surprise saw that the room was full of furniture, not covered in dustsheets as I had expected, but just as though it were in use. There were brushes and combs on the dressing table. The bed was made up. There were flowers. Shoes were neatly positioned in front of a chair. For one strange moment I thought that something had happened to my brain, that I was seeing back in time and looking at the room as it used to be, before she died . . . In a minute, Rebecca herself would come back into the room, sit down at her dressing table, reach for her comb and start running it through her hair. I went on standing there, waiting for something to happen. It was the sound of the clock that brought me back to reality again. The hands stood at twenty-five past four. My watch said the same. It reminded me that tea would soon be ready under the trees. No – this room was not used. It was not lived in any more. Even if Mrs Danvers did put the flowers on the tables and the sheets on the bed, they would not bring Rebecca back. She was dead. She had been dead for a year now. She lay buried below the church, with all the other dead de Winters.

But yes, it was a beautiful room. Mrs Danvers had told the truth that first evening. It was the most beautiful room in the house. I touched the sheets; on the bed was a nightdress, cold now, but still carrying a woman's faint and lovely smell. I looked round with a growing feeling of disgust, disgust turning to hopelessness.

Then I heard a step behind me and, turning round, I saw Mrs Danvers. I shall never forget the look on her face – evil, excited in a strange, unhealthy way. I felt very frightened.

'Is anything the matter, madam?' she said.

I tried to smile and could not. I tried to speak.

'Are you feeling unwell?' she asked, coming near to me, speaking very softly. I felt her breath on my face.

'I'm all right, Mrs Danvers,' I said, after a moment. 'I didn't expect to see you.'

'You wanted to see the room? Why have you never asked me to show it to you before? You only had to ask me.'

I wanted to run away, but I could not move. I went on watching her eyes.

'Now you are here, let me show you everything,' she said, her voice sweet and false. 'I know you want to see it all – you've wanted to for a long time, but didn't like to ask. It's a lovely room, isn't it? The loveliest room you have ever seen. This is her bed; here is her nightdress. You have been touching it, haven't you? Feel – how soft and light it is! This is the nightdress she was wearing the night before she died. She was wearing trousers, of course, and a shirt when she was drowned. They were torn from her body in the water, though. There was nothing on the body when it was found, all those weeks afterwards.' Her fingers tightened on my arm, her face was close, her dark eyes searching mine. 'The rocks had knocked her to pieces, you know; her beautiful face was unrecognizable, and both arms gone. Mr de Winter went up to Edgecoombe. He went quite alone. He was very ill at the time, but he was determined to go. No one could stop him – not even Mr Crawley.' She paused, her eyes never leaving my face. 'I shall always blame myself for the accident,' she said. 'It was my fault for being out that evening. I had gone into Kerrith for the afternoon and stayed there late, as Mrs de Winter was up in London and wasn't expected back until much later. That's why I didn't hurry back. When I came in, about half past nine, I heard she had returned, then had dinner and gone out again. Down to the boat, of course. I felt worried then. The wind was blowing from the south-west. She would never have gone if I had been in. She always listened to me.' Her fingers held me tightly, hurting my arm. 'Mr de Winter had been dining with Mr Crawley down at his house,' she went on. 'I don't know what time he got back. I expect it was after eleven. But it began to blow hard before midnight, and she had not come back. I went and knocked on the bedroom door. Mr de Winter answered immediately. "Who is it? What do you want?" In a moment he opened the door, wearing his night clothes. "She's spending the night down at the cottage, I expect," he said; "I should go to bed if I were you. She won't come back here to sleep if the storm goes on like this." He looked tired, and I did not want to disturb him again. After all, she spent many nights at the cottage, and was used to sailing in any weather. She might not even have gone for a sail, but just wanted a night at the cottage, as a change after London. I said good night to Mr de Winter and went back to my room. I couldn't sleep, though. I kept wondering what she was doing.'

She paused again. I did not want to hear any more. I wanted to get away from her, away from the room.

'You know now why Mr de Winter doesn't use these rooms any more. Listen to the sea! He hasn't used these rooms since the night she was drowned. Sometimes when Mr de Winter is away and you feel lonely, you might like to come up to these rooms and sit here. You only have to tell me.' Her smile was a false, unnatural thing. 'They are such beautiful rooms. You wouldn't think she had been gone so long, would you, by the way the rooms are kept? You would think she had just gone out for a little while and would be back in the evening. It's not only in this room – it's in many rooms in the house. In the sitting room, the hall, the little flower room. I feel her everywhere. You do, too, don't you?' She paused, watching my eyes. 'Do you think she can see us, talking to one another now? Do you think the dead come back and watch the living?'

I swallowed. 'I don't know.' My voice sounded high, unnatural. Not my voice at all.

'Sometimes I wonder,' she whispered. 'Sometimes I wonder if she comes back to Manderley and watches you and Mr de Winter together.'

We stood there, watching one another. I could not take my eyes away from hers. How dark they were, how full of hatred! Then she opened the door and stepped to one side for me to pass. 'Tea is ready now,' she said. 'They have orders to take it out under the trees.'

◆

Next day, in Beatrice's car, I wondered whether to tell her about Mrs Danvers. About the man Favell.

'Beatrice,' I said, deciding that I would, 'have you ever heard of someone called Favell? Jack Favell?'

'Jack Favell,' she repeated. 'Yes, I do know the name. Wait a minute. Jack Favell? Yes, of course. A terrible man! I met him once, years ago.'

'He came to Manderley yesterday, to see Mrs Danvers,' I said.

'Really? Oh, well – perhaps he would . . .'

'Why?'

'I believe he was Rebecca's cousin.'

I was very surprised. That man her relation? It was not my idea of the sort of cousin Rebecca would have. Jack Favell her cousin. 'Oh,' I said. 'I hadn't realized that.'

'He probably used to go to Manderley a lot. I don't know. I couldn't tell you. I was very rarely there.' I felt she didn't want to talk about him.

'I didn't like him much,' I said.

'No,' said Beatrice. 'I don't blame you.'

I waited, but she did not say any more.

When I got back to Manderley, Maxim's hat was lying on the table. As I went towards the library, I heard the sound of voices, one raised louder than the other – Maxim's voice. The door was shut, and I paused.

'You can write and tell him from me to keep away from Manderley in future, do you hear? Never mind who told me; I happen to know that his car was seen here yesterday afternoon. If you want to meet him, you can meet him outside Manderley. I won't have him inside the gates, do you understand? Remember – I'm warning you – for the last time!'

I moved quickly away. Mrs Danvers came out of the library. She did not see me, but for a moment I saw her face, grey with anger, twisted, horrible.

I waited a moment, then I went in. Maxim was standing by the window, holding some letters in his hand, his back turned to me.

'Who is it now?' he said.

I smiled, holding out my hands. 'Hullo!' I said.

'Oh, it's you . . .'

I could see that something had made him very angry. His mouth was hard, his face white. We sat down together by the window.

'Was it hot up in London?'

'Yes, quite bad. I always hate the place.'

I wondered if he would tell me what had happened just now with Mrs Danvers. I wondered who had told him about Favell.

'Are you worried about something?'

'I've had a long day. That drive twice in twenty-four hours is too much for anyone.' He got up and wandered away, lighting his pipe. I knew then that he was not going to tell me about Mrs Danvers.

Chapter 6 The Fancy-Dress Dance

It was one Sunday, I remember, when we had visitors, that the subject of the fancy-dress dance was first brought up. Maxim's eyes met mine over the teapot.

'What do you think?' he said.

'I don't know,' I said uncertainly. 'I don't mind.'

'I think everyone would enjoy a show of some sort,' said Frank.

Maxim still looked at me doubtfully over the teapot. Perhaps he thought I could not manage it. I did not want him to think that. I did not want him to think I would let him down.

'I think it would be rather fun,' I said.

'That settles it, of course. All right, Frank. Go ahead with the arrangements. Better get Mrs Danvers to help you. She'll remember how we used to do things.'

'I've got the records in the office. It won't really mean much work. Mrs de Winter needn't worry about anything.' I wondered what they would do if I suddenly said that I would take charge of the whole affair. Laugh, I suppose, and then begin talking of something else.

'What on earth shall I wear?' I said. 'I'm not much good at fancy dress. I tell you what, I'll keep my choice a surprise until the last minute. Then I'll give you and Frank the surprise of your lives.'

◆

The preparations went on for the dance. Maxim and Frank were busy every morning and I began to worry about what I was going to wear. It seemed so silly not to be able to think of anything. One evening, when I was changing for dinner, there was a knock at my bedroom door. I called 'Come in,' thinking it was my servant, Clarice. It was Mrs Danvers.

'I hope you will forgive me disturbing you,' she said. 'Have you decided yet, madam, what you will wear?'

There was a suggestion of scorn in her voice, of strange satisfaction. She must have heard through Clarice that I still had no ideas.

'No. I haven't decided.'

'Why don't you copy the clothes from one of the pictures in the hall?'

'Yes. I might think about that.' I wondered why such an idea had not come to me before. It was an obvious solution to my problem.

'All the pictures in the hall would be easy to copy, especially that one of the young lady in white, with her hat in her hand.' Her voice was surprisingly normal. Did she want to be friends with me at last? Or did she realize that it was not I who had told Maxim about Favell, and was this her way of thanking me for my silence? 'Has Mr de Winter not suggested anything for you?'

'No. No, I want to surprise him and Mr Crawley.'

'When you do decide, I would advise you to have your dress made in London. Voce, in Bond Street, is a good place I know. I should study the pictures in the hall, madam, especially the one I mentioned. And you needn't think that I'll give you away. I won't say a word to anyone.'

'Thank you, Mrs Danvers.' I went on dressing, confused by her manner, and wondering if I had the unpleasant Favell to thank for it.

When I looked at the picture, I saw that the clothes in it were lovely, and would be easy to copy. It was a painting by Raeburn of Caroline de Winter, who had been a famous London beauty in the eighteenth century. She wore a simple white dress. The hat might be rather difficult, but I could carry it in my hand, as she did. I would have to wear a hairpiece. My hair would never curl in that way. Perhaps Voce in London would do the whole thing. It was a relief to have decided at last.

◆

Clarice could hardly contain herself for excitement, and I began to feel the same as the great day came near. Beatrice and her husband were coming to stay the night, and a lot of other people were coming to dinner before the dance began.

I found Clarice waiting for me in my room, her round face red with excitement. We laughed at each other like schoolgirls. The dress fitted perfectly.

'It's lovely, madam – fit for the Queen of England!'

'Give me the curls carefully. Don't spoil them.' With trembling fingers I made the finishing touches. 'Oh, Clarice, what will Mr de Winter say?' I did not recognize the face that I saw in the mirror. The eyes were larger, surely, the mouth thinner, the skin white and clear? The curls stood away from the head in a little cloud. I watched this self that was not me at all, and then smiled; a new, slow smile.

'They've gone down,' said Clarice. 'They're all standing in the hall. Mr de Winter, Captain and Mrs Lacy, and Mr Crawley.' I went along the passage and looked down, hidden from view at the top of the stairs.

'I don't know what she's doing,' Maxim was saying, 'she's been up in the bedroom for hours.'

The band were near me, getting their instruments ready.

'Make the drummer give a roll on the drum,' I whispered, 'and then shout out "Miss Caroline de Winter".' What fun it was! Suddenly the sound of the drum filled the great hall; I saw them look up, surprised.

'Miss Caroline de Winter!' shouted the drummer.

I came forward to the top of the stairs and stood there, smiling, my hat in my hand like the girl in the picture. I waited for the laughter and shouts of approval that would follow as I walked slowly down the stairs. Nobody moved. They all stared at me, speechless. Beatrice gave a little cry and put her hand to her mouth. I went on smiling.

'How do you do, Mr de Winter?' I said.

Maxim had not moved. He looked up at me, his glass in his hand. All the colour left his face. I stopped, one foot on the next stair. Something was wrong. They had not understood. Why was Maxim looking like that? Why did they all stand as if they were made of stone?

Then Maxim moved forward, his eyes never leaving my face.

'What the devil do you think you are doing?' His eyes flashed with anger. His face was ash grey. I could not move.

'It's the picture,' I said. 'It's the picture – the one in the hall.'

There was a long silence. We went on looking at each other. Nobody moved in the hall. I swallowed; my hand moved to my throat. 'What is it?' I said. 'What have I done?'

If only they wouldn't look at me like that with dull, expressionless faces. If only somebody would say something. When Maxim spoke again, I did not recognize his voice. It was quiet, cold as ice – not a voice I knew.

'Go and change,' he said. 'It doesn't matter what you put on. Find an ordinary evening dress – anything will do. Go now, before anybody else comes.'

I could not speak. I went on looking at him. His eyes were the only living things in his dead, grey face.

'What are you standing there for?' His voice was ugly and strange. 'Didn't you hear what I said?'

I turned and ran blindly down the passage behind me. Clarice had gone. Tears filled my eyes. Then I saw Mrs Danvers. I shall never forget the expression on her face – the face of a victorious devil. She stood there, smiling at me. And then I ran from her, down the long passage to my own room.

◆

Somebody knocked. The door opened and Beatrice came in.

'My dear! Are you all right? You look very white. Of course I knew immediately it was just a terrible mistake. You couldn't possibly have known. Why should you?'

'Known what?'

'Why the dress, you poor dear – the picture you copied of the girl in the hall. It was what Rebecca did at the last fancy-dress dance at Manderley. Exactly the same. The same picture, the same dress. You stood there on the stairs, and for one terrible moment I thought . . . You poor child, how were you to know?'

'I ought to have known,' I said stupidly. 'I ought to have known.'

'Nonsense – how could you? It was not the sort of thing that could possibly enter any of our heads. Only it was such a shock, you see. We none of us expected it, and Maxim . . .'

'Yes, Maxim?'

'He thinks, you see, you did it on purpose. You had said you would surprise him, hadn't you? Some foolish joke. And, of course, he doesn't understand. It was such a shock for him. I told him that you couldn't have done such a thing on purpose, and that it was just bad luck that you chose that particular picture.'

'I ought to have known. It's all my fault. I ought to have known!'

'No, no. Don't worry. You'll be able to explain the whole thing to him quietly. Everything will be all right. The first lot of people are just arriving. I've told Frank to make up a story of your dress not fitting, and how disappointed you are.'

I did not say anything. I went on sitting on the bed. I kept seeing Maxim's eyes in his grey face, and the others behind him, not moving, just staring at me.

Chapter 7 The Sunken Boat

It seemed to me the next morning, as I lay in bed, staring at the wall, at the faint light coming in at the window, at Maxim's empty bed, that there was nothing quite so shaming as a marriage that had failed. Failed after three months, as mine had done. For I no longer made any effort to pretend. Last night had shown me too well. My marriage was hopeless. We were not companions. I was too young for Maxim, too inexperienced, and more important still, I was not of his world. Even Mrs Van Hopper had known it. 'I'm afraid you'll be sorry. I believe you're making a big mistake.' I would not listen to her; I thought she was hard and cruel. But she was right. 'Don't imagine that he's in love with you! He's lonely. He can't bear that great empty house, that's all.' It was true! Maxim was not in love with me; he had never loved me. He did not belong to me at all, he belonged to Rebecca. She was in the house still, as Mrs Danvers had said, and he would never love me, because of her.

Outside, low clouds of mist hung around the windows. Thick and white, they smelt of the salty sea. I could see nothing out of

36

the windows; everything was hidden in mist and silence.

Suddenly an explosion shook the windows. It was followed by another, and another. The birds rose unseen from the woods and filled the air with their noise. I heard the sound of footsteps running below. It was Maxim. I could not see him, but I could hear his voice.

'There's a ship in trouble,' he was saying. 'She's signalling for help. She must have mistaken our bay for Kerrith harbour. The mist is as thick as anything out there. If she's on the rocks, they'll never move her. I'm going down to see if I can do anything.'

It was getting warmer. A pale sun was trying to shine, and the heavy mist was lifting. When I reached the shore the mist had almost gone, and I could see the ship, lying about three kilometres out, with some small rowing boats already around her. In a dark grey motorboat was the harbour master from Kerrith. Another motorboat followed, full of holidaymakers. I climbed up the path over the cliff. I did not see Maxim there, but Frank was talking to one of the coastguards, a man I had met before.

'Come to see the fun, Mrs de Winter? I'm afraid it will be a difficult business. They may move her, but I doubt it. She's stuck on those rocks.'

'What will they do?'

'They'll send a diver down now to see if she's broken her back.'

A small boy came running up to us. 'Will the sailors be drowned?' he asked.

'Not them! They're all right, son,' said the coastguard. 'The sea's as flat as the back of my hand. No one's going to be hurt this time. There's the diver, Mrs de Winter! See him?'

'I want to see the diver,' said the small boy.

'There he is,' said Frank, bending down and pointing. 'They're going to lower him into the water.'

'Won't he be drowned?'

'Divers don't drown. They have air pumped down to them all

the time. Watch him disappear. There he goes!'

'He's gone,' said the small boy.

'Where's Maxim?' I asked.

'He's taken one of the sailors into Kerrith, to the doctor. I don't suppose anything will happen now for hours. The diver will have to make his report before they try to move her. I want my lunch. Why not come back and have some with me?'

'I think I'll stay here a bit. I want to see what the diver's going to do.' Somehow I could not face Frank at the moment. I wanted to be alone.

◆

It was after three o'clock when I looked at my watch. I got up and went down the hill to the bay. It was quiet and deserted as always. When I came to the further side of the bay I saw Ben sitting by a rock pool.

'Good day,' he said, his wet mouth opening in a smile.

'Good afternoon,' I replied.

He stood up. 'Seen the ship?'

'Yes. She's in trouble, isn't she?'

'Eh?'

'She's on the rocks. I expect she's got a hole in her.'

His face looked empty and foolish. 'Yes,' he said. 'She's down there all right. She'll not come back again.'

'Perhaps they'll get her off when the tide comes in.'

He did not answer. He was staring out towards the ship. 'She'll break up, where she is.'

'I'm afraid so.'

He smiled again, and wiped his nose with the back of his hand. 'She'll break up bit by bit. She'll not sink like a stone, like the little one.' He laughed quietly to himself. I did not say anything. 'The fishes have eaten her up by now, haven't they?'

'Who?' I said.

'Her. The other one.'

'Fishes don't eat boats, Ben,' I said.

'Eh?' he said. He stared at me, foolish and dull once more.

'I must go home now,' I said. 'Good afternoon.'

I left him, and walked up the path through the woods to the house.

Just as I was having tea, Robert came in.

'Mr de Winter isn't back yet, is he, madam?'

'No,' I said. 'Does someone want him?'

'Yes, madam. It's Captain Searle, the harbour master from Kerrith. He says the matter is rather urgent. He tried to get Mr Crawley, but there was no reply.'

'Well, of course I must see him, if it's important.'

I wondered what I would say to Captain Searle. It must be something to do with the ship. I could not understand what concern it was of Maxim's.

I got up and shook hands with him when he came in. 'I'm sorry my husband isn't back yet, Captain Searle. I'm afraid the ship has disorganized everybody. Will they get her off, do you think?'

Captain Searle made a great circle with his hands. 'There's a hole that big in her,' he said. 'She'll not see home again. But never mind the ship – her owner and the insurance company will settle that between them. No, Mrs de Winter, it's not the ship that's brought me here. The fact is, I have some news for Mr de Winter, and I hardly know how to tell it to him.' He looked at me very straight with his bright blue eyes.

'What sort of news, Captain Searle?'

He brought a large white handkerchief out of his pocket and blew his nose. 'Well, Mrs de Winter, it's not very pleasant for me to tell you, either. The last thing I want to do is to cause pain to you or your husband. We're all very fond of Mr de Winter in Kerrith, you know, and the family has always done a lot of good.

It's hard on him and it's hard on you that we can't let the past lie quiet. But I don't see how we can.' He paused, and put his handkerchief back in his pocket. He lowered his voice, although we were alone in the room.

'We sent the diver down to examine the ship's bottom; he found the hole, and was working his way round to see what other damage there was, when he came across a little sailing boat, lying on her side, quite whole and not broken up at all. He's a local man, of course, and he recognized the boat immediately. It was the little boat belonging to the first Mrs de Winter.'

'I'm so sorry,' I said slowly, 'it's not the sort of thing one expected would happen. Is it necessary to tell Mr de Winter? Couldn't the boat be left there as it is? It's not doing any harm, is it?'

'It *would* be left, Mrs de Winter, in the ordinary way. I'd give anything, as I said before, to spare Mr de Winter's feelings. But that wasn't all, Mrs de Winter. He found the door tightly closed, and the windows, too. But he broke one of the windows with a piece of rock, and looked inside. It was full of water; it must have come in through some hole in the bottom. There seemed to be no damage elsewhere. And then he got the fright of his life, Mrs de Winter.'

Captain Searle paused; he looked over his shoulder as though one of the servants might hear him. 'There was a body in there, lying on the floor. There was no flesh left on it, but it was a body all right . . . And now you understand, Mrs de Winter, why I've got to see your husband.'

I kept looking at him, confused at first, then shocked, then rather sick.

'She was supposed to be sailing alone,' I whispered, 'there must have been someone with her all the time then, and no one ever knew.'

'It looks like it.'

40

'Who could it have been? Surely relatives would know if anyone was missing? There was so much in the papers about it. Why should one of them be still in the boat and Mrs de Winter be found many kilometres away, and months afterwards?'

Captain Searle shook his head. 'I can't tell. All we know is that the body is there, and it has got to be reported. It's very hard on you and Mr de Winter. Here you are, settled down quietly, wanting to be happy, and now this has to happen. But I've got to do my duty. I've got to report that body.' He stopped as the door opened and Maxim came into the room.

'Hullo — what's happening? I didn't know you were here, Captain Searle. Is anything the matter?'

I could not stand it any longer. I went out of the room, like the coward I was, and shut the door behind me.

When I heard the sound of a car starting up the drive, I went slowly back to the library. Maxim was standing by the window. He did not turn round. I reached for his hand.

'I'm so sorry — so terribly, terribly sorry.'

His hand was icy cold. He did not answer.

'I don't want you to bear this alone,' I said. 'I want to share it with you. I've grown up, Maxim, in twenty-four hours.'

He put his arm round me and pulled me close.

'You've forgiven me, haven't you?'

He spoke to me at last. 'Forgiven you?' he said. 'What have I got to forgive you for?'

'Last night,' I said. 'You thought I did it on purpose.'

'Ah, that,' he said. 'I'd forgotten. I was angry with you, wasn't I?' He did not say any more. He went on holding me.

'Maxim,' I said, 'can't we start all over again? Can't we begin from today, and face things together?'

He took my face between his hands and looked at me. For the first time I saw how thin his face was, how lined and tired. There were great shadows beneath his eyes.

41

'It's too late, my love, too late. We've lost our little chance of happiness.'

'No, Maxim, no,' I said.

'Yes. It's all over now. The thing has happened.'

'What thing?'

'The thing I have always expected. The thing I have dreamed about, night after night. We were not meant for happiness, you and I.'

'What are you trying to tell me?'

He put his hands over mine and looked into my face. 'Rebecca has won,' he said.

I stared at him, my heart beating strangely, my hands suddenly cold beneath his hands.

'Her shadow was between us all the time — her shadow keeping us from one another. I remember her eyes as she looked at me before she died. I remember that last slow smile. She knew this would happen even then. She knew she would win in the end.'

'Maxim,' I whispered, 'what are you saying? What are you trying to tell me?'

'Her boat,' he said. 'They've found it — the diver found it this afternoon.'

'Yes, I know,' I said. 'Captain Searle came to tell me. You're thinking about the body, aren't you — the body the diver found in it?'

'Yes.'

'It means she was not alone. It means there was somebody sailing with Rebecca at the time. And you have to find out who it was. That's it, isn't it, Maxim?'

'No,' he said. 'No. You don't understand.'

'I want to share this with you, Maxim. I want to help you!'

'There was no one with Rebecca. She was alone.'

I did not move. I watched his face.

'It's Rebecca's body lying there in the boat,' he said.

'No,' I said. 'No.'

'The woman buried below the church is not Rebecca. It's the body of some unknown woman, unclaimed, belonging nowhere. There never was an accident. Rebecca was not drowned at all. I killed her. I shot Rebecca in the cottage in the bay. I carried her body to the boat, and sailed it out that night and sank it there, where they found it today. It's Rebecca who's lying dead there on the floor in the boat. Will you look into my eyes and tell me that you love me now?'

◆

It was very quiet in the library. When people suffer a great shock, like death, or the loss of an arm or a leg, I believe they do not feel it at first. If your hand has gone, you don't know for a few minutes. You go on feeling the fingers. You stretch them and move them one by one and all the time there is nothing there – no hand, no fingers. I, too, felt no pain, no fear, there was no horror in my heart. Little by little, feeling will come back to me, I thought; little by little I shall understand. What he has told me will fall into place and I will understand. They will fit themselves into a pattern. At the moment I am nothing. I have no heart, no mind, no senses. I am just a wooden thing in Maxim's arms.

'What will they do?' I said, stupidly.

'They will know it's her body. Everything is there – the shoes, the rings on her fingers. Then they will remember the other one – the woman buried below the church.'

'What are you going to do?' I whispered.

'I don't know,' he said. 'I don't know.'

The feeling was coming back to me, little by little, as I knew it would. My hands were no longer cold. I felt a wave of colour come into my face. Maxim had killed Rebecca. Rebecca had not been drowned at all. Maxim had killed her. He had carried her

43

body to the boat, and sunk the boat there in the bay. I began to understand . . . Maxim's silence. The way he never talked about Rebecca. His dislike of the little bay, of the stone cottage. 'If you had my memories you would not go there either.' The way he went so quickly up the path through the woods, not looking behind him. 'I came away in rather a hurry,' he said to Mrs Van Hopper, with that look on his face. 'They say he can't get over his wife's death.' The fancy-dress dance last night, and I coming to the head of the stairs, in Rebecca's dress. 'I killed Rebecca,' Maxim had said. 'I shot Rebecca in the cottage.' And the diver had found her lying there, on the floor of the boat.

'What are we going to do?' I said. 'What are we going to say?'

Maxim did not answer. He stood there by the fireplace, his eyes wide and staring, looking in front of him, not seeing anything.

'Does anyone know? Anyone at all?'

He shook his head. 'No.'

'No one but you and me?' I thought for a moment. 'Frank!' I said suddenly. 'Are you sure Frank doesn't know?'

'How could he? There was nobody there but myself. It was dark . . .' He stopped. He sat down in a chair, he put his hand up to his forehead. I went and knelt beside him. He sat very still. I took his hand from his face and looked into his eyes. 'I love you,' I whispered. 'I love you. Will you believe me now?' He kissed me, and held my hands very tightly, like a child needing comfort.

'I thought I would go mad,' he said, 'sitting here, day after day, waiting for something to happen. Eating and drinking, trying to seem natural in front of Frith, the servants, Mrs Danvers – whom I had not the courage to turn away, because with her knowledge of Rebecca she might have guessed – Frank, always by my side, and poor, dear Beatrice. I had to face them, all those people, knowing that every word I said was a lie.'

'Why didn't you tell me? The time we've wasted when we might have been together! All those weeks . . .'

'You were so distant,' he said, 'always wandering into the garden with Jasper, going off on your own. You never came to me like this.'

'Why didn't you tell me?' I whispered. 'Why didn't you tell me?'

'I thought you were unhappy, bored. I'm so much older than you. You always had more to say to Frank than to me. You were strange with me – awkward.'

'How could I come to you, when I knew you were thinking of Rebecca? How could I ask you to love me when I knew you still loved Rebecca?'

He pulled me close to him and searched my eyes.

'What are you talking about? What do you mean?'

'Whenever you touched me I thought you were comparing me with Rebecca. Whenever you spoke to me or looked at me, walked with me in the garden, sat down to dinner, I felt that you were saying to yourself, "This I did with Rebecca, and this, and this."' He stared at me as if he did not understand.

'It was true, wasn't it?' I said.

'Oh, my God,' he said. He pushed me away, and began walking up and down the room.

'What is it? What's the matter?'

He turned suddenly and looked at me as I sat there on the floor. 'You thought I loved Rebecca? You thought I killed her, loving her? I hated her, I tell you. Our marriage was a lie from the very first. She was a terrible woman; every bone in her body was bad. We never loved each other; never had one moment of happiness together. Rebecca had no love, no warmth. She was clever, of course – very clever. No one would guess that she was not a kind, generous and caring person. She knew exactly what to say to everyone. If she had met you, she would have walked off into the garden with you, arm-in-arm, talking about flowers, music, painting, whatever she knew you were interested in, and you would have been deceived like the rest. You would have loved her. When I married her, I was told I was the luckiest man in the world. She was so lovely, so intelligent, so amusing. But all the time I had a seed of doubt at the back of my mind. There was something about her eyes . . .'

Bit by bit the real Rebecca took shape in front of me. Once more I stood on the beach with poor Ben. 'You're not like the other one. She gave you the feeling of a snake . . .'

Maxim was talking, though, walking up and down the library. 'I discovered her true nature immediately,' he was saying, 'five days after we were married. She told me about herself – told me things I shall never repeat to a living soul. I knew then what I had done, what I had married. She made a deal with me. "I'll run your house for you," she told me. "I'll look after your dear old Manderley for you – make it the most famous showplace in the country, if you like. And people will visit us, and be jealous of us, and talk about us; they'll say we are the happiest, luckiest, best-looking pair in England. What a joke, Max!" she said, laughing. "What a great joke!" She knew I would give up pride, honour, personal feelings, everything, rather than stand before our little world after a week of marriage and have them know the things about her that she had told me then. I thought too much of Manderley. I put Manderley first, before anything else. And it isn't right, that sort of love. They don't speak about it in the churches. They don't speak about stones, and bricks, and walls, the love that a man can feel for his bit of earth, his home and castle.'

'Maxim, my love!'

'Do you understand?' he said. 'Do you? Do you?'

'Yes,' I said. But I looked away from him so that he did not see my face. What did it matter whether I understood? My heart was as light as a feather. He had never loved Rebecca.

'I don't want to look back on those years. The misery, the disgust. The lie we lived, she and I. In front of friends, relations,

46

even the servants. They all believed in her down here, they all admired her. They never knew how she laughed at them behind their backs. I can remember days when the place was full for some entertainment or other – a dance, or a garden party – and she walked around with her arm through mine; then the next day she would be up at daybreak driving to London, to that flat of hers by the river like an animal to its hole in the ground, coming back here at the end of the week, after five unspeakable days. Oh, I kept my part of the deal all right. I never gave her away. And her good taste made Manderley what it is today. The gardens, the sitting room, even the flowers in the Happy Valley – the beauty of Manderley that people talk about and photograph and paint, it's all because of her, because of Rebecca.'

I did not say anything. I held him close. I wanted him to talk, so that his bitterness would come out, carrying with it all the hatred and disgust of those lost years.

'And so we lived, month after month, year after year. I accepted everything – because of Manderley. What she did in London did not touch me – because it did not hurt Manderley. And she was careful at first; there was never a whisper about her. Then she began to ask her friends down here. She would have them at her cottage in the bay. I told her she must keep to her part of the deal. She could see her friends in London, but Manderley was mine. She smiled, but said nothing. Then she started on Frank – poor pitiful Frank, who had not understood, who had always thought we were the normal happy pair we had pretended to be.

'I accused Rebecca, and we had a terrible, sickening scene. She went up to London after that, and stayed there a month. I thought she had learned her lesson. Then we had Beatrice and Giles for the weekend, and I realized then what I had sometimes thought before, that Beatrice did not like Rebecca. I believe she saw through her, guessed that something was wrong. Giles went out sailing with Rebecca, and when they came back I could see that

47

she had started on him, as she had done on Frank.'

All the pieces were fitting into place for me now – Frank's awkward manner when I spoke about Rebecca. Beatrice's strange attitude. The silence I had always taken for sympathy was a silence of shame and embarrassment. It seemed unbelievable now that I had never understood. I wondered how many people there were who suffered because they could not break out from their own self-consciousness and awkwardness. I had never had the courage to demand the truth. If I had taken one step, Maxim would have told me these things months ago.

'Rebecca became careful again,' he went on. 'Her behaviour was faultless. But if I happened to be away when she was here at Manderley, I could never be certain what might happen. There had been Frank, and Giles. She might get hold of one of our workmen, someone from Kerrith, anyone . . . and then the blow would fall. The talk, the shame I feared.

'She had a cousin who had been abroad, but was living in England again. He began coming here, if ever I was away. A man called Jack Favell.'

'I know him; he came here the day you were in London.'

'You saw him too? Why didn't you tell me? I heard it from Frank, who saw his car turn in at the gates.'

'I thought it would remind you of Rebecca,' I said.

'Remind me?' whispered Maxim. 'As if I needed reminding.' He paused, and I wondered if he was thinking, as I was, of that flooded boat beneath the waters in the bay.

'She used to have this Favell down to the cottage,' said Maxim. 'She would tell the servants she was going to sail and would not be back before the morning. Then she would spend the night down there with him. Once again I warned her. I said if I found him here, anywhere in the grounds, I'd shoot him . . . The very thought of him walking around the woods at Manderley, in places like the Happy Valley, made me mad. I told her I would not stand

48

it. Then one day she went up to London and came back again the same day, which she did not usually do. I did not expect her. I had dinner that night with Frank at his house.

'I returned after dinner at about half past ten, and I saw her things in the hall. I wondered what the devil she had come back for. But she was not there. I guessed she had gone off again – down to the bay. And I knew I could not stand this life of lies and deceit any longer. I thought I'd take a gun and frighten him, frighten them both. I went straight down to the cottage. The servants never knew I had come back to the house at all. I slipped out into the garden and through the woods. I saw a light in the cottage window, and went straight in. To my surprise Rebecca was alone. She looked ill, strange.

'I began immediately to talk to her about Favell. "This is the end, do you understand? What you do in London does not concern me. You can live with Favell there, or with anyone you like. But not here. Not at Manderley."

'She said nothing for a moment. She looked at me, and then she smiled. "Suppose it suits me better to live here? What then?"

'"You know the conditions," I said. "I've kept my part of our miserable deal, haven't I? But you've cheated. You think you can treat my house and my home like your own hole in London. I've had enough, and my God, Rebecca, this is your last chance."'

'She stretched herself, her arms above her head.

'"You're right, Max," she said. "It's time I changed." She looked very pale, very thin. She began walking up and down, her hands in her pockets.

'"Have you ever thought," she said, "how hard it would be for you to make a case against me? In a court of law, I mean. Do you realize that you wouldn't have a hope of proving anything? All your friends – even the servants – believe our marriage to be a success."'

'"What about Frank? What about Beatrice?"'

'She threw back her head and laughed. "What sort of a story do you think Frank could tell, against mine? As for Beatrice – wouldn't it be the easiest thing in the world to show her to be an ordinary jealous woman whose husband once lost his head and made a fool of himself? Oh, no, Max – you'd have a difficult time trying to prove anything against me." She stood watching me, her hands in her pockets and a smile on her face. "Do you realize that I could get Danny to swear anything I asked her to swear? And that the rest of the servants would follow her? They think we live together at Manderley as husband and wife, don't they? And so does everyone, your friends, all our little world. Well, how are you going to prove that we don't?"

'She sat down on the edge of the table, swinging her leg, watching me. "Haven't we acted the parts of a loving husband and wife rather too well?" she said. I remember watching that foot of hers, swinging backwards and forwards, and my eyes and brain began to burn. "We could make you look very foolish, Danny and I," she said softly. "We could make you look so foolish that no one would believe you, Max, nobody at all." Still that foot of hers was swinging backwards and forwards. Suddenly she slipped off the table and stood in front of me, smiling still, her hands in her pockets. "If I had a child, Max, neither you nor anyone in the world could prove that it was not yours. It would grow up here in Manderley, bearing your name. There would be nothing you could do. And when you died, Manderley would be his. You could not prevent it. You would like that, wouldn't you? You would enjoy it, seeing my son asleep under the trees, playing on the grass, picking flowers in the Happy Valley? You would love watching my son grow bigger day by day, and knowing that when you died, all this would be his?"

'After a minute she went to the window. She began to laugh. She went on laughing. I thought she would never stop. "God, how funny! How beautifully funny! Well, you heard me say I was going to change, didn't you? Now you know the reason. They'll be happy, won't they, all the people here? 'It's what we've always hoped for, Mrs de Winter,' they'll say. I'll be the perfect mother, Max, as I've been the perfect wife. And none of them will ever guess, none of them will ever know."

'She turned round and faced me, smiling, one hand in her pocket. When I killed her she was smiling still. I fired at her heart. The bullet passed right through her. She did not fall immediately. She stood there looking at me, with that slow smile on her face, her eyes wide open . . .

'I had to get water from the bay,' Maxim continued. 'I had to keep going for more. There was blood all round where she lay on the floor. The wind began to blow harder, too. There was no hook on the window. It kept banging backwards and forwards, while I knelt there on the floor with that cloth, and the bucket of water beside me.

'I carried her to the boat. It must have been half past eleven by then, or nearly twelve. It was quite dark. There was no moon, the wind was blowing hard at times, from the west. I carried her below and left her there. Then I had to sail out of the little harbour against the tide, with the rowing boat behind me. It was difficult. It was blowing all right, but I was sheltered by the cliffs. I remember I got the sail stuck. I hadn't sailed, you see, for a long time. I never went out with Rebecca. But I got the boat out into the bay, beyond the cliff. I tried to turn her, to get well away from the rocks. Suddenly the wind blew harder; it tore the rope from my hands. The sail began to thunder and shake. I couldn't remember what one had to do – I couldn't remember. I tried to reach the rope, but it was like a whip in the air above my head. The wind was coming from in front of us, and we were being blown back. It was dark – so dark that I couldn't see anything on the black, slippery boat. Somehow I got down below. I had a heavy tool in my hand. If I didn't do something now, it would be too late! Being blown like this, we would soon be out of deep water. I drove the pointed tool into the bottom boards. It was heavy; it split one of the boards right across. I pulled it out and drove the point into another board. Then another. The water came up over my feet. I left Rebecca there on the floor, and shut the windows and the door. When I came back up I saw how near the shore we had been driven by the wind. I climbed into the rowing boat, and watched. She was sinking. The sails were still banging about, and I thought someone would hear – someone walking on the cliffs late at night, or some fishermen from Kerrith whose boat I could not see. Her nose was sinking first. Then she turned over onto her side. Suddenly she was not there any more. I remember staring at the place where she had been. Then I rowed back to the harbour. It started to rain.'

Maxim stopped, still staring straight in front of him. Then he turned to me.

'That's all,' he said, 'there's no more to tell. I walked up the path through the woods. I went into the house. I remember undressing. It was blowing and raining hard, off and on. I was sitting there on the bed when Mrs Danvers knocked on the door. I went and opened it, in my night clothes, and spoke to her. She was worried about Rebecca, but I told her to go back to bed. I shut the door again. I went back and sat by the window, watching the rain, listening to the sea down in the bay.'

◆

We sat there together without saying anything. I went on holding his cold hands.

'She sank too close in,' said Maxim. 'I meant to take her right out into the bay. They would never have found her there.'

'It was the ship. They would never have found her if it were not for the ship.'

'She sank too close in,' Maxim repeated.

52

We were silent again. I began to feel very tired.

'I knew it would happen one day,' said Maxim. 'It was only a question of time. Finding you has not made any difference, has it? Loving you does not change things at all. Rebecca knew she would win in the end. I saw her smile, when she died.'

'Rebecca's dead. She can't harm you any more.'

'There's her body. The diver has seen it. It's lying there, on the floor of the boat.'

'We've got to explain it. We've got to. It must be the body of someone you don't know. Someone you have never seen before.'

'Her things will still be there,' he said. 'The rings on her fingers. Even if her clothes have decayed in the water, there will be something there to tell them. It's not like a body lost at sea, beaten against the rocks.'

'How will you find out? How will you know?'

'The diver is going down again at five in the morning. Searle has made all the arrangements. They are going to try to raise the boat. No one will be around. I'm going with them.'

'And then?'

'Searle is going to try to get her back to Kerrith and put her on the mud halfway up Kerrith harbour. He'll get the water out of her. He's going to get hold of a doctor.'

'If they find out it's Rebecca, you must say the other body in the church was a mistake – a terrible mistake. You must say that when you went up to Edgecoombe you were ill, you didn't know what you were doing. You weren't sure, even then. You will say that, won't you?'

'Yes,' he said. 'Yes.'

'They can't prove anything against you,' I said. 'Nobody saw you that night. You had gone to bed. They can't prove anything. No one knows but you and I. No one at all. Not even Frank. We are the only two people in the world to know, Maxim. You and I.'

'Yes,' he said. 'Yes.'

'They'll think the boat turned over and sank when Rebecca was down below; they'll think she went below for a rope or something, and while she was there the wind came across the bay, and the boat turned over, and Rebecca was trapped. They'll think that, won't they?'

'I don't know,' he said. 'I don't know.'

Suddenly the telephone began ringing in the little room behind the library.

Maxim went in and shut the door. Robert came in to take away the tea. I stood up, my back to him, so that he wouldn't see my face. I wondered when they would know – how long it would take for the news to spread. When Robert had gone, Maxim came back into the room.

'It was Colonel Julyan. He's just been talking to Searle. He's coming out to the boat with us tomorrow.'

'Why Colonel Julyan? Why?'

'He's the Justice of the Peace★ for Kerrith. He has to be present.'

'What did he say?'

'He asked me if I had any idea whose body it would be. I said I didn't know. I said we believed Rebecca to be alone. I said I didn't know of any friend.'

'Did he say anything after that?'

'He asked me if I thought it possible that I made a mistake when I went up to Edgecoombe.'

'He said that? He said that already?'

'Yes.'

'And you?'

'I said it might be possible. I didn't know.'

'He'll be with you there tomorrow, when you look at the boat? He, and Captain Searle, and a doctor?'

★ Justice of the Peace: a person who judges cases in a local law court.

'Inspector Welch, too.'

'Inspector Welch!'

'Yes.'

'Why Inspector Welch?'

'It's the custom when a body has been found.' He looked quickly out of the window. 'The wind has died away again.'

'Yes,' I said.

'It will be a flat calm tomorrow for the diver,' he said.

We dressed for dinner as usual. Afterwards we went back to the library. We did not talk much – I sat on the floor at Maxim's feet, my head against his knees. There were no shadows between us any more. I wondered how I could be so happy when the little world about us was so black. It was a strange sort of happiness. Not what I had dreamed about. There was nothing feverish or urgent about it. It was a quiet, still happiness. The library windows were wide open and we looked out at the dark, dull sky.

◆

At about half past eleven the next morning there was a message that Maxim was bringing Frank and Colonel Julyan to lunch.

The morning dragged slowly on. It was very hot. I went upstairs and changed into a thinner dress. Then I sat and waited. At five minutes to one I heard the sound of a car in the drive, and voices. I stood up, waiting for them to come into the room. In the mirror, my face looked very pale. Maxim came in, and Frank and Colonel Julyan.

'How do you do?' Colonel Julyan said. He spoke seriously and quietly, like a doctor.

'Give Colonel Julyan a drink,' said Maxim, 'we are just going to wash.'

Colonel Julyan did not have anything to drink. I took some, to give me something to hold. He came and stood beside me at the window.

'This is a most disturbing thing, Mrs de Winter,' he said gently. 'I do feel for you and your husband very much.'

'Thank you,' I said. I put my glass down on the table. I was afraid that he would notice that my hand was shaking.

'What makes it so difficult is your husband saying he recognized the first body at Edgecoombe, over a year ago.'

'I – I don't quite understand.'

'You didn't hear, then, what we found this morning?'

'I knew there was a body. The diver found a body.'

'Yes.' Then, looking over his shoulder towards the door, 'I'm afraid it was her, without a doubt. I can't go into details, but both your husband and Dr Phillips were sure.'

He stopped suddenly and moved away from me. Maxim and Frank had come back into the room.

'Lunch is ready; shall we go in?' said Maxim.

As we drank our coffee, Colonel Julyan started again in his quiet way – I looked steadily at my plate. 'I was saying to your wife before lunch, de Winter, that the awkward part of this whole business is the fact that you said you recognized that original body.'

'I think the mistake was very natural,' said Frank quickly. 'It was suggested that the body was hers when he was asked to go up to Edgecoombe. Besides, Maxim was not well at the time. I wanted to go with him, but he was determined to go alone. He was not in a fit state to decide anything of the sort.'

'That's nonsense,' said Maxim. 'I was perfectly well.'

'Well, it's no good going into all that now. You recognized the body, and now the only thing to do is to admit your mistake. There seems to be no doubt about it this time. I wish you could be spared a public inquiry, but I'm afraid that's quite impossible. It needn't take very long. It's just a matter of your saying you recognize the body, and then getting Tabb, the boatbuilder, to say that the boat was in good order when he last had her in his yard.

56

No, what worries me is the noise the newspapers will make about it. So sad and unpleasant for you and your wife.'

'That's quite all right,' said Maxim. 'We understand.'

'So unfortunate, that ship getting into trouble there. But for that, the whole matter would have rested in peace. The only thing is, we now know that Mrs de Winter's death must have been sudden – not the slow affair we imagined it to be. No question of trying to swim.'

'None,' said Maxim.

'She must have gone below for something, and then the door stuck, and suddenly a strong wind caught the boat with nobody on the lookout. That seems to be the solution, don't you think, Crawley?'

'Oh, yes – undoubtedly,' said Frank.

I looked up, and saw Frank looking at Maxim. He turned away again immediately, but not before I had seen and understood the expression in his eyes. Frank knew. And Maxim did not know that he knew. I went on drinking my coffee. My hand holding the cup was hot and wet.

'I suppose sooner or later we all make a mistake in judgment,' said Colonel Julyan. 'Mrs de Winter must have known how the wind comes round the cliff in that bay; it wasn't safe to leave a small boat like that and go down below. She must have sailed alone over that spot many times. Then, just once, she took a chance – and the chance killed her.'

'Accidents happen so easily,' said Frank, 'even to the most experienced people.'

'Yes. But if Mrs de Winter hadn't gone below, the accident would never have happened. A strange thing to do. I never knew her to make a mistake in a boat. That was the sort of thing only a beginner would do.'

'It was blowing hard that night. Something may have got stuck. And then she slipped down for a knife.'

'Of course. Of course. Well, we shall never know. As I said, I wish I could stop the inquiry, but I can't. It will be as short as possible. But I'm afraid we shan't be able to keep the newspaper reporters out of it.'

I did not look at Frank when he said goodbye; I was afraid he would understand my eyes. I did not want him to know that I knew.

When they had gone, Maxim said: 'It's going to be all right. I'm quite confident. You saw how Julyan was at lunch, and Frank. There won't be any difficulty at the inquiry. It's going to be all right.'

I did not say anything. I held his arm tightly.

'There was never any question of the body being someone unknown. It was quite obvious this morning. What we saw was enough for Dr Phillips to recognize her, even without me. There was no sign of what I had done. The bullet had not touched the bone. You heard what they said; they think she was trapped there, down below. They will believe that at the inquiry, too. Dr Phillips will tell them.'

He paused. Still I did not speak.

'I only mind for you,' he said. 'If it had to come all over again, I would not do anything different. I'm glad I killed Rebecca. I shall never be sorry for that, never, never. But you! I can't forget what it has done to you. It's gone for ever, that funny, young, lost look that I loved. It won't come back again. I killed that, too, when I told you about Rebecca . . . It's gone, in twenty-four hours. You are so much older . . .'

◆

It was in all the papers the next day. Pictures of Maxim, and of Manderley. They described Rebecca as beautiful, clever, popular, and Maxim as marrying again the following spring and bringing his young wife to Manderley, giving a big fancy-dress dance for her, and then the next morning the body of his first wife being found, trapped in her sailing boat at the bottom of the bay. It made a good story.

I thought of all the things they could say, if they knew the truth. All over the front page. Newsboys shouting in the streets. That terrible six-letter word printed large and black . . .

Frank came up after breakfast. He looked pale and tired, as though he had not slept. 'I've told them to put all telephone calls for Manderley through to the office,' he said. 'If those newspapermen ring up, I can deal with them.'

'Those reporters!'

'We all want to kick them, but you've got to see their point of view. It's their job. But you won't have to see them or speak to them, Maxim. All you have to think about is your statement at the inquiry.'

'I know what to say.'

'Of course you do. But don't forget that old Horridge will be in charge. He's an awkward sort of man. Likes to go into details just to show how thorough he is. You mustn't let him worry you.'

'Why the devil should I be worried? I have nothing to be worried about.'

'Of course not. But I've been to these inquiries before, and it's easy to get annoyed. You don't want to lose your temper.'

'Frank's right,' I said. 'I know just what he means. The more quickly and smoothly the whole thing goes, the easier it will be for everyone. Then, once it's over, we'll forget all about it, and so will everyone else, won't they, Frank?'

'Yes, of course,' said Frank.

I still avoided his eye, but I was surer than ever that he knew the truth. He had always known it. From the very beginning.

Chapter 8 The Inquiry

On the way to the inquiry Maxim was quite calm. It was like going with someone to hospital — someone who was going to have an operation — and not knowing what would happen, not knowing whether the operation would be successful. My hands were very cold. My heart was beating strangely. When we got there, I decided not to go in, but to wait outside in the car.

It was early-closing day. The shops looked dull and there were very few people about. I sat looking at the silent shops as the minutes went by. I wondered what was happening. I got out of the car, and began walking up and down. Somehow, without wanting to, I came to the building where the inquiry was being held.

A policeman appeared from nowhere.

'You can't wait here.'

'I'm sorry,' I said, turning away.

'Oh, excuse me, madam; of course, you're Mrs de Winter, aren't you? You can wait in here if you like.'

He showed me into a small empty room, like a waiting room at a railway station. I sat there. Five minutes passed and nothing happened. It was worse than being outside in the car. I got up and went into the passage. The policeman was standing there.

'How long will they be?'

'I'll go and inquire, if you like.'

In a moment he was back again. 'I don't think they'll be very much longer,' he said. 'Mr de Winter has just made his statement. Captain Searle, the diver and Dr Phillips have given theirs. There's only one more to speak. Mr Tabb, the boatbuilder.'

'Then it's nearly over?'

'I expect so, madam. Would you like to hear the rest of it? There's a chair just inside the door. If you slip in now, nobody will notice you.'

'Yes,' I said. 'Yes. I think I will.'

I followed the policeman, slipped in, and sat down just by the door. The room was smaller than I had imagined, and very hot. There were people there that I did not know; I looked at them out of the corner of my eye. My heart gave a jump suddenly as I recognized Mrs Danvers. And Favell was beside her. Jack Favell, Rebecca's cousin. I had not expected him to be there. James Tabb, the boatbuilder, was standing up now, answering questions.

'Was the boat in a fit state to put to sea?'

'She was when I fixed her up in April of last year. That would be Mrs de Winter's fourth season with the boat.'

'Had the boat ever been known to turn over before?'

'No, sir. I should soon have heard from Mrs de Winter if there had been any question of it. She was pleased with the boat in every way, from what she said to me.'

'I suppose great care was needed in handling the boat?'

'Well, sir, everyone has to be careful, sailing a boat, it's true. But this one was a strong, well-built boat, and could stand a lot of wind. Mrs de Winter had sailed her in worse weather than that night. Why, it was only blowing now and again. That's what I said all along. I couldn't understand her boat going down on a night like that.'

'But, surely, if Mrs de Winter went below for a coat, as is supposed, and a sudden strong wind were to come round that cliff, it would be enough to turn the boat over?'

James Tabb shook his head. 'No. I don't believe that it would.'

'Well, I'm afraid that's what must have happened. I don't think Mr de Winter or any of us suggest that you were to blame at all. You fixed the boat up at the beginning of the season, you say she was in good condition, and that's all I want to know. It seems that Mrs de Winter was careless for a moment, and she lost her life, the boat sinking with her on board. Such things have happened before. I repeat, we are not blaming you.'

'Excuse me, sir,' said the boatbuilder, 'but there's a bit more to it than that. And if you'll allow me, I'd like to make a further statement.'

'Very well. Go on.'

'It's like this, sir. After the accident last year, a lot of people in Kerrith said I had let Mrs de Winter start the season in a damaged boat that let the water in. I lost some work because of it. It was very unfair, but the boat had sunk, and there was nothing I could say to defend myself. Well, I went to have a look at her yesterday. I wanted to satisfy myself that the work I had done was all right.'

'Well, that was very natural. I hope you were satisfied.'

'Yes, sir, I was. There was nothing wrong with my work. I examined it all. She'd sunk onto sand. I asked the diver about that, and he told me so. She hadn't touched the rocks. They were one and a half metres away. She was lying on sand, and there wasn't the mark of a rock on her.'

He paused.

'Well? Is that all you want to say?'

'No. It's not. What I want to know is this. Who made the holes in her? Rocks didn't do it. The nearest rock was one and a half metres away. Besides, they weren't the sort of holes made by a rock. They were made with some pointed tool. On purpose.'

I did not look at him. I looked at the floor. It was hot – much too hot. Why didn't they open a window? I wondered why no one said anything. Why did the silence last so long?

'What do you mean? What holes?' The voice sounded very far away.

'There were three of them. Driven through her with something sharp. With those holes in her, it wouldn't take long for a small boat like her to sink. Not ten minutes, I should say. Those holes were not there when the boat left my boatyard. It's my opinion, sir, that the boat never turned over at all. She was sunk on purpose.'

I must try to get out of the door. There was no air in the place . . . They were talking. Someone in front of me was standing up, and I couldn't see anything. It was hot, so very hot. Maxim was standing up now. I could not look at him.

'Mr de Winter, you heard the statement from James Tabb. Do you know anything of these holes in the boat?'

'Nothing at all.'

'Mr de Winter, I want you to believe that we all feel for you in this matter. No doubt you have suffered a shock, a great shock, in learning that your wife was found in her boat, and not at sea, as you supposed. I am inquiring into the matter for you. I want to find out exactly how and why she died. James Tabb has just said that the boat had three holes hammered through her bottom. Do you doubt his statement?'

'Of course not. He's a boatbuilder. He knows what he's talking about.'

'Who looked after Mrs de Winter's boat?'

'She looked after it herself.'

'She employed no man to help her?'

'No, nobody at all.'

'The boat was kept in the private harbour at Manderley?'

'Yes.'

'Any stranger who tried to damage the boat would be seen? There is no public footpath to the harbour?'

'No.'

'Yet James Tabb has told us that a boat with those holes hammered in her probably could not float for more than ten minutes.'

'Yes.'

'So that the boat cannot have been damaged before Mrs de Winter took her out, or she would have sunk in the harbour?'

'No doubt.'

'Therefore we must suppose that whoever took the boat out

that night made the holes in her?'

'Yes.'

'You have told us already that the door was shut, the windows also, and your wife's remains were on the floor. This was in your statement, and in Doctor Phillips's, and in Captain Searle's.'

'Yes.'

'And now comes the statement that with some sharp instrument three holes had been made in the bottom. Does this not strike you as very strange?'

'Certainly.'

'You have no suggestion to make?'

'None at all.'

'Mr de Winter, painful as it may be, it is my duty to ask you a very personal question. Were the relations between you and your first wife perfectly happy?'

It was hot, so hot, with all these people. No open window. The door was further away than I had thought, and all the time the ground coming up to meet me.

And then came Maxim's voice, clear and strong: 'Will someone take my wife outside? She's going to faint.'

Chapter 9   Favell Accuses Maxim

I was sitting in the little room again – the room like a waiting room at a station. The policeman was there, giving me a glass of water, and someone's hand was on my arm, Frank's hand. I sat quite still, the floor, the walls, Frank and the policeman coming into place in front of me.

'I'm so sorry,' I said. 'Such a stupid thing to do. It was so hot in that room.'

'It gets very airless in there,' said the policeman. 'We've had ladies fainting in there before.'

'Are you feeling better, Mrs de Winter?' said Frank.

'Yes. Yes. Much better: I shall be all right now. Don't wait with me.'

'I'm going to take you back to Manderley.'

'No!'

'Yes. Maxim has asked me to.'

'I want to wait for him.'

'Maxim may be a long time.'

Why did he say that? What did he mean? Why didn't he look at me? He took my arm and walked with me down the steps into the street. Maxim may be a long time . . .

We did not speak. We drove away towards Manderley.

'Why will they be a long time? What are they going to do?'

'They may have to go over the facts again.'

'They've had all the facts. There's nothing more anyone can say.'

'You never know. Tabb's statement has changed everything. They may have to do it in a different way.'

'What way? What do you mean?'

'You heard what Tabb said about the boat? They won't believe it was an accident now.'

'It's all wrong, Frank! They shouldn't listen to Tabb. How can he tell, after all these months, how holes were made in the boat? What are they trying to prove?'

'I don't know.'

'They'll go on questioning Maxim, making him lose his temper, making him say things he doesn't mean. They'll ask question after question, Frank, and Maxim won't be able to stand it. I know he won't stand it!'

Frank did not answer. He was driving very fast. That meant he was worried, very worried.

'That man was there – that man who came to Manderley to see Mrs Danvers.'

'You mean Favell? Yes, I saw him.'

'He was sitting there with Mrs Danvers.'

'I know.'

'Why was he there? What right had he to go?'

'He was her cousin.'

'It's not right that he and Mrs Danvers should sit there, listening. I don't trust them, Frank.'

'No.'

'They might do something; they might make trouble.'

Again Frank did not answer. I realized that he was too loyal to Maxim to be drawn into a discussion, even with me. He did not know how much I knew. We were friends, we travelled the same road, but we dared not look at one another. Neither of us dared risk saying what we knew.

In my room, I lay down on my bed. Perhaps they would question Frank as well – ask him about that evening, over twelve months ago, when Maxim had had dinner at his house. The exact time that Maxim left. Whether anybody saw Maxim when he got back to Manderley. Whether anyone could prove that Maxim went straight upstairs to bed. Mrs Danvers might be called on. She might be questioned. And Maxim beginning to lose his temper, beginning to turn white ...

I must have fallen asleep, because I woke suddenly at the first crack of thunder. I sat up. The hands on the clock were pointing to five. I went to the window. There was not a breath of wind. The leaves hung still, waiting. The sky was grey. More thunder in the distance. No rain fell. I went down to the library and at half past five Robert came in.

'The car has just driven up to the door now, madam.'

'Which car?'

'Mr de Winter's car, madam.'

'Is Mr de Winter driving it himself?'

'Yes, madam.'

I tried to get up, but my legs were weak; they would not hold me up. I stood leaning against a chair. My throat was very dry. After a minute Maxim came in. He stood just inside the door.

He looked tired, old. There were lines at the corners of his mouth I had never noticed before.

'It's all over,' he said.

I waited. Still I could not speak or move towards him.

'She killed herself . . . they were all in the dark, of course. They didn't know what to do.'

'Killed herself?' I sat down on the chair. 'But why?'

'Goodness knows! They did not seem to think it necessary to decide. Old Horridge, going on at me – wanting to know if Rebecca had any money troubles. Money troubles!'

He went and stood by the window, looking out at the green grass. 'It's going to rain. Thank God, it's going to rain at last.'

'What happened? What did Horridge say? Why have you been there all this time?'

'He went over and over the same ground again,' said Maxim. 'Little details about the boat that nobody cared about. I thought I would go mad. I kept my temper, though. Seeing you there by the door made me remember what I had to do. If you hadn't fainted like that, I would never have done it. The shock reminded me, and then I knew exactly what I had to say. I never took my eyes off old Horridge – I shall remember his face until my dying day. I'm so tired I can't see or hear or feel anything.'

He sat down, his head in his hands. I went and sat beside him.

'Where's Frank?' I asked.

'He had to go to the church. I would have gone, too, but I wanted to come straight back to you. I kept thinking of you, waiting, all by yourself, not knowing what was going to happen.'

'Why the church?'

'We have to do something there this evening.'

Then I understood. They were going to bury Rebecca.

'It's fixed for half past six. There won't be anybody hanging about. It was arranged yesterday. The inquiry doesn't make any difference.'

He looked tired, so deathly tired.

'I wish you didn't have to go out again,' I said.

'It won't take long.'

'I'll come with you. I shan't mind. Let me come with you.'

'No. I don't want you to come.'

Then he left me, and I heard the sound of the car becoming fainter. Just after seven the rain began to fall. Gently at first, and so lightly that I could not see it. Then louder and faster. I left the windows wide open, stood in front of them and breathed the cold, clean air. The rain fell on my face and hands. It came down thick and fast, so that I could not even see the trees.

I did not hear Frith come in at the door.

'Excuse me, madam, but do you know if Mr de Winter will be long?'

'No. Not very long.'

'There's a gentleman to see him, madam.' He paused. 'I'm not quite sure what I ought to say. He's determined to see Mr de Winter.'

'Who is it? Anyone you know?'

Frith looked uncomfortable. 'Yes, madam. It's a gentleman who used to come here frequently at one time. A Mr Favell.'

I turned and shut the window. The rain was coming in on the cushions. Then I looked at Frith. 'I think perhaps I had better see Mr Favell,' I said.

'Very good, madam.'

I went and stood beside the empty fireplace. It was just possible that I would be able to get rid of Favell before Maxim came back. I did not know what I was going to say to him, but I was not frightened.

In a few moments Frith showed him in. He looked rather untidy. His eyes looked red. I wondered if he had been drinking.

'I'm afraid Maxim isn't here,' I said. 'I don't know when he will be back. Wouldn't it be better if you saw him at the office in the morning?'

'Waiting doesn't worry me,' said Favell, 'and I don't think I shall have to wait very long. I had a look in the dining room as I came along, and I see Max is expected to dinner all right.'

'Our plans have been changed; it's quite possible that Maxim won't be home at all this evening.'

'He's run off, has he?' said Favell with a half-smile I did not like. 'I wonder if you really mean it! Tell me, are you feeling better? Too bad, fainting like that this afternoon. I would have come to help, but I saw you had someone to help you. I expect Frank Crawley enjoyed himself. Did you let him drive you home? You wouldn't let me drive you five metres!'

'What do you want to see Maxim about?'

'You've grown up a bit since I saw you last, haven't you? I wonder what you've been doing? I don't think I shall mind very much if Max *doesn't* get back to dinner! What do you say?'

'Mr Favell,' I said, 'I don't want to be rude, but I'm very tired – I've had a long day. If you can't tell me what you want to see Maxim about, it's not much good your sitting here. You had far better do as I suggest, and go round to the office in the morning.'

'No. No. No. Don't run away and leave me! I'm quite harmless, really I am. And I think you are behaving very well over this, really very well. I take my hat off to you – I really do.' His speech was very thick. I wished I had never told Frith I would see him.

'You come down here to Manderley,' he said, waving his arm rather wildly, 'you take on all this place, meet hundreds of people you've never seen before, you put up with old Max and his temper, you don't give in to anyone, you just go your own way. I call it a good effort, and I don't care who hears me say so. A good effort.' He steadied himself against the table. 'This business has

69

been a shock to me, you know. A terrible shock. Rebecca was my cousin. I was very fond of her. Always great friends. Liked the same things, the same people. Laughed at the same jokes. I suppose I was fonder of Rebecca than of anyone else in the world. And she was fond of me. All this has been a great shock.'

'Yes,' I said. 'I'm very sorry for you.'

'And what is Max going to do about it? That's what I want to know. Does he think he can sit back quietly now that the inquiry is over? Tell me that.' He was not smiling any more. He bent towards me. 'I'm going to see that justice is done for Rebecca. Killed herself!' He leaned closer to me. 'You and I know she didn't, don't we?' He leaned closer to me still. 'Don't we?' he said slowly.

The door opened and Maxim came into the room, with Frank just behind him. Maxim stood quite still, with the door open. 'What the devil are you doing here?' he said.

Favell turned, his hands in his pockets. Then he began to smile. 'As a matter of fact, Max, old man, I came to congratulate you on the result of the inquiry this afternoon.'

'Do you mind leaving the house?' said Maxim. 'Or do you want Crawley and me to throw you out?'

'Steady a moment, steady a moment!' said Favell. He sat down on the arm of a chair. 'You don't want Frith to hear what I'm going to say, do you? Well, he will, if you don't shut that door.'

Maxim did not move. I saw Frank close the door very quietly.

'Now listen here, Max,' said Favell, 'you've come out of this affair very well, haven't you? Oh yes, I was at the inquiry this afternoon. I was there from start to finish – I saw your wife faint, at a rather important moment, and I don't blame her. It could have gone either way for you, Max, couldn't it? And lucky for you that it went the way it did. You realize, don't you, Max old man, that I can make things very unpleasant for you if I choose. Not only unpleasant, but – shall I say – dangerous?'

Still Maxim did not move. He never took his eyes off Favell.

'Oh yes?' he said. 'In what way can you make things dangerous?'

'Look here, Max, you know all about Rebecca and me. We were lovers, weren't we? I've never lied about it. Very well then. Up to now I believed, like every other fool, that Rebecca was drowned sailing in the bay, and that her body was picked up at Edgecoombe, weeks afterwards.' He paused, and sat there, looking at each one of us in turn. 'Then I picked up the evening paper a few days ago and read that Rebecca's boat had been found, and that there was a body down below. I couldn't understand it. Who would Rebecca have as a sailing companion? It didn't make sense. I came down here and stayed at a hotel. I got in touch with Mrs Danvers. She told me that the body was Rebecca's. Even so, I thought, like everyone else, that the first body was a mistake, and that Rebecca had somehow got shut in when she went down to get a coat. Well, I went to the inquiry today, as you know. And everything went smoothly, didn't it, until Tabb spoke? But after that? Well, Max, old man, what have you got to say about those holes hammered in the bottom of the boat?'

'Do you think,' said Maxim slowly, 'that after all those hours of talk this afternoon I am going through it again – with you? You heard the inquiry. That must satisfy you.'

'Killed herself, eh? Rebecca killed herself? The sort of thing she would do, was it? Listen; you never knew I had this note, did you? I kept it, because it was the last thing she ever wrote to me. I'll read it to you. I think it will interest you.'

He took a piece of paper out of his pocket. ' "I tried to telephone you from the flat," ' he read, ' "but could get no answer. I'm going down to Manderley right away. I shall be at the cottage this evening, and if you get this in time, will you get the car and follow me? I'll spend the night at the cottage, and leave the door open for you. I've got something to tell you and I want to see you as soon as possible. Rebecca." ' He put the note back in his pocket. 'That's not the sort of note you write when you're going to kill yourself, is it? It was waiting for me at my flat when I got back at about four in the morning. I had no idea Rebecca was going to be in London that day, or I would have got in touch with her. As it was, I was at a party that night. When I read the note I decided it was too late to start driving for six hours down to Manderley. I went to bed, determined to put through a call later in the day. I did. And I learnt that Rebecca had been drowned!'

He sat there, looking at Maxim.

'Supposing I had produced that note at the inquiry this afternoon, it would have been awkward for you, wouldn't it, Max, old man?'

'Well – why didn't you?'

'Steady, old boy. No need to get worried! You've never been a friend to me, but I don't mind. All married men with lovely wives are jealous, aren't they? I don't blame them. Now, Max, I've laid all my cards on the table. Why can't we come to some agreement? I'm not a rich man – I'm too fond of taking risks for that. But what worries me is not having anything in the bank to fall back on. Now, if I had a settlement of two or three thousand pounds a year for life I could get along quite comfortably. And I'd never trouble you again. I swear I wouldn't.'

'I've asked you to leave the house,' said Maxim. 'I'm not going to ask you again. There's the door. You can open it yourself.'

'Half a minute, Maxim,' said Frank, 'it's not quite so easy as that.' He turned to Favell. 'I see what you're after. It happens, unfortunately, that you could twist things round and make it difficult for Maxim. I don't think he sees that as clearly as I do. What is the exact amount you suggest that Maxim should settle on you?'

I saw Maxim go white. 'Don't get involved with this, Frank,' he said, 'this is my affair. I'm not going to give way to threats. You think you can frighten me, don't you, Favell? Well, you're wrong. I'm not afraid of anything you can do. Shall I ring up Colonel Julyan and ask him to come over? He's the Justice of the Peace. He'll be interested in your story.'

Favell looked hard at him, then he laughed.

'A good try,' he said, 'but it won't work. You wouldn't dare ring up old Julyan! I've enough here to hang you, Max, old man.'

Maxim walked slowly across the library, and into the little room beyond.

'Stop him!' I said to Frank. 'Stop him, please!'

Frank went over to him quickly. I heard Maxim's voice, very cool, very calm. 'I want Kerrith 17,' he said. Favell was watching the door. 'Leave me alone!' I heard Maxim say to Frank. Then – 'Is that Colonel Julyan? It's de Winter here. Yes. Yes, I know. I wonder if you could possibly come over to Manderley immediately? It's rather urgent. I can't explain why, on the telephone, but you'll hear everything when you come. I'm sorry to have to drag you out. Yes. Thank you very much, goodbye.'

He came back again into the room. 'Julyan is coming now,' he said. He went to the windows and threw them open. It was still raining very hard. He stood there with his back to us, breathing the cold air. We none of us said anything. There was no sound but the falling rain. I felt helpless. There was nothing I could do. I had to sit there, watching the rain.

It was raining too hard to hear the car. We did not know Colonel Julyan had arrived until the door opened, and Frith showed him in.

'I think you realize,' Maxim said, 'that I haven't brought you out on an evening like this for a social half-hour before dinner. This is Jack Favell, my first wife's cousin. Go ahead, Favell.'

Favell got up. The short wait seemed to have calmed him. He was not smiling any longer. I had the feeling that he was not too pleased at the way things had happened, and was not ready for

Colonel Julyan. He began speaking in a loud and unpleasant voice. 'Look here, Colonel Julyan, I'll come straight to the point. The reason why I'm here is that I am not satisfied with the result of the inquiry this afternoon.'

'Oh?' said Colonel Julyan. 'Isn't that for de Winter to say?'

'No, I don't think it is. I have a right to speak, not only as Rebecca's cousin, but as the man she would have married, if she had lived.'

Colonel Julyan looked very surprised. 'I see. Is this true, de Winter?'

'It's the first I've heard of it,' said Maxim.

Colonel Julyan looked from one to the other doubtfully. 'Look here, Favell,' he said, 'what exactly is your trouble?'

Favell stared at him a moment. I could see that he was planning something in his mind, but had had too much to drink to be able to carry it out. He put his hand in his pocket and brought out Rebecca's note. 'This note was written a few hours before Rebecca is supposed to have set out to kill herself at sea. Here it is. Read it, and say whether you think the woman who wrote that note had made up her mind to kill herself.'

Colonel Julyan read the note. Then he handed it back. 'No. On the face of it, no. But I don't know what she was going to tell you. Perhaps you do – or perhaps de Winter does?'

Maxim said nothing.

'My cousin made a definite appointment in that note, didn't she? She clearly asked me to drive down to Manderley that night because she had something to tell me. She made the appointment, and she was to spend the night in the cottage on purpose to see me alone. The fact of her going for a sail does not surprise me – it was the sort of thing she did after a long day in London. But to hammer holes in the floor of the boat and drown herself – oh no, Colonel Julyan, by God no!' The colour had flooded into his face, and the last words were shouted.

I could see that Colonel Julyan did not like Favell. 'My dear man, it's not the slightest use your losing your temper with me. You say you refuse to believe that your cousin killed herself. But you heard what the boatbuilder said. The holes were there. Suppose we get to the point. What do you suggest really happened?'

Favell turned his head and looked slowly towards Maxim. He was twisting the note between his fingers. 'Rebecca never made those holes. She never killed herself. Rebecca was murdered. And if you want to know who the murderer is, there he stands, by the window there! He couldn't even wait, could he, until a year had passed, before marrying the first girl he set eyes on. There's your murderer for you, Mr Maximilian de Winter. Take a long look at him. He'd look well hanging, wouldn't he?'

And Favell began to laugh, the laugh of a man who had been drinking, high and foolish, all the time twisting Rebecca's note between his fingers.

Thank God for Favell's laugh. Thank God for his pointing finger, his red face, his wild eyes. Thank God for the way he stood there, rocking slightly on his feet. It put Colonel Julyan on our side.

'The man's been drinking,' he said quietly. 'He doesn't know what he's saying.'

'Been drinking, have I?' shouted Favell. 'Oh, no, my fine friend. You may be a Justice of the Peace and a colonel too, but that means nothing to me. I've got the law on my side, for a change, and I'm going to use it. There are other Justices of the Peace besides you. Men with brains in their heads. Max de Winter murdered Rebecca, and I'm going to prove it.'

'Wait a minute, Mr Favell,' said Colonel Julyan quietly, 'you were at the inquiry this afternoon. If you felt so deeply about it, why didn't you produce that letter in court?'

Favell looked hard at him, then laughed. 'Because I didn't

choose to, that's why. I preferred to come and deal with de Winter personally.'

'That's why I asked you to come here,' said Maxim, walking forward from the window. 'I asked him the same question. He said he was not a rich man, and that if I cared to settle two or three thousand a year on him for life he would never worry me again. Frank was here, and my wife. They both heard him. Ask them.'

'It's perfectly true, sir,' said Frank.

'Mr Favell,' said Colonel Julyan. 'You have just made a serious accusation against Mr de Winter. Have you any proof?'

'Proof?' said Favell. 'What the devil do you want with proof? Aren't those holes in the boat proof enough?'

'Certainly not, unless you can produce a witness who saw him do it. Where's your witness?'

'Witness! Who else would kill Rebecca? I tell you de Winter killed Rebecca because of me. He knew I was her lover; he was madly jealous. He knew she was waiting for me at the cottage, and he went down that night and killed her. Then he put her body in the boat and sank it.'

'Quite a clever story, Favell, in its way, but you have no proof. Produce a witness who saw it happen, and I might begin to take you seriously.'

'Wait a minute,' said Favell, 'wait a minute . . . There's quite a good chance that de Winter might have been seen that night.'

I suddenly knew what Favell meant. And in a flash of fear and horror I knew that he was right. Little sentences came back to me. 'She's down there all right. She'll not come back again.' 'The fishes have eaten her up by now, haven't they?' Ben had seen! Ben, with his poor, foolish brain, had been a witness all the time.

'There's a local man who spends his time on the shore. He was often around when I was down there with Rebecca. He used to sleep in the woods in hot weather. The man's a fool, and would

76

never have come forward on his own. But I can make him talk if he did see anything that night, and there's a good chance he did.'

'He must mean Ben,' said Frank, with a quick look at Maxim. 'He's the son of one of our men. But he's not responsible for what he says or does. He's not very intelligent.'

'What the devil does that matter?' said Favell. 'He's got eyes, hasn't he? He knows what he sees. He's only got to answer yes or no.'

'Can we get hold of this man and question him?' asked Colonel Julyan.

'Of course. Drive down to his mother's cottage, Frank, and bring him back. We want to end this thing, don't we?'

◆

The door opened, and Frank came in. He turned and spoke to someone in the hall outside.

'All right, Ben,' he said quietly. 'There's nothing to be frightened of.'

Ben came awkwardly into the room. He looked strange without his hat. I realized for the first time that he had no hair. He looked different, horrible. The light seemed to confuse him. He looked foolishly round the room.

Then Favell walked towards him. 'Hullo,' he said, 'how has life treated you since we last met?'

Ben looked at him, giving no sign that he recognized him. He did not answer.

'Well?' said Favell. 'You know who I am, don't you?'

'Eh?'

'You know who I am, don't you?'

Colonel Julyan walked across to him. 'You shall go home in a few minutes, Ben. No one's going to hurt you. We just want you to answer one or two questions. You know Mr Favell, don't you?'

This time Ben shook his head. 'I never seen him,' he said.

'Don't be a fool; you know you've seen me! You've seen me go to the cottage on the shore. Haven't you?'

'No,' said Ben. 'I never seen no one.'

'A useful witness!' said Colonel Julyan.

Favell swung round on him. 'Someone has got at this fool and paid him. I tell you he's seen me lots of times.'

'I never seen you,' said Ben. Then he took hold of Frank's arm. 'Has he come to take me to the madhouse? I don't want to go to the madhouse. They're cruel to people in there. I want to stay at home. I done nothing.'

'That's all right, Ben,' said Colonel Julyan. 'No one's going to put you in the madhouse. Now, you remember the lady who had the boat?'

'She's gone.'

'Yes, we know that. She used to sail the boat, didn't she? Were you on the shore when she sailed it the last time – when she didn't come back again?'

'Eh?'

'You were there, weren't you?' said Favell. 'You saw Mrs de Winter come down to the cottage, and later you saw Mr de Winter, too. He went into the cottage after her. What happened then? Go on. What happened?'

Ben drew back against the wall. 'I seen nothing. I want to stay at home. I'm not going to the madhouse. I've never seen you. Never before.' He began to cry like a child.

'Your witness doesn't seem to have helped you,' said Colonel Julyan.

'He's been paid,' shouted Favell. 'Paid to tell his string of lies.'

Frank took Ben out of the room. 'The man seemed to be frightened,' said Colonel Julyan to Maxim. 'I was watching him. He's never been treated badly, has he?'

'No,' said Maxim. 'He's perfectly harmless. I've always let him do as he pleased.'

'He's been frightened at some time,' said Colonel Julyan. 'He was showing the whites of his eyes – just like a dog does when you're going to whip him.'

'Well, why didn't you?' said Favell. 'He'd have remembered me all right if you had whipped him.'

'He hasn't helped you, has he?' said Colonel Julyan. 'You say you were going to marry Mrs de Winter, and that you used to meet her secretly in the cottage. You can't even prove *that* story, can you?'

'Can't I?' said Favell. I saw him smile. He came across to the fireplace and rang the bell.

I guessed what was going to happen. Frith answered the bell. 'Ask Mrs Danvers to come here,' said Favell. Then he turned to Colonel Julyan. 'Mrs Danvers was Rebecca's personal friend. She was with her for years before she married. You will find her a very different sort of witness from Ben.'

Frank looked quickly at Maxim. Colonel Julyan saw the look, and his lips tightened. I did not like it.

We all waited, watching the door. Mrs Danvers came into the room and stood by the door, her hands folded in front of her, looking from one to the other of us.

'First of all, Mrs Danvers, I want to ask you a question,' said Colonel Julyan. 'Did you know of the relationship between the late Mrs de Winter and Mr Favell here?'

'They were cousins,' said Mrs Danvers.

'I mean something closer than that.'

'I'm afraid I don't understand, sir.'

'Oh, nonsense, Danny!' said Favell. 'You know what he means. You know Rebecca and I had lived together on and off for years, hadn't we? She was in love with me, wasn't she?'

Mrs Danvers looked at him for a moment: 'She was not.'

'Listen to me, you old –' began Favell, but Mrs Danvers cut him short. 'She was not in love with you, or with Mr de Winter. She

79

was not in love with anyone. She hated men. She was above all that.'

Favell said angrily: 'Now, listen. Didn't she come through the woods to meet me, night after night? Didn't you wait up for her? Didn't she spend the weekends with me in London?'

'Well,' said Mrs Danvers with sudden anger, 'and what if she did? She had a right to amuse herself, hadn't she? Lovemaking was a game with her – only a game. She told me so. She did it because it made her laugh. It made her laugh, I tell you! She laughed at you as she laughed at all the rest. I've known her come back and sit upstairs in bed and rock with laughter at the lot of you.'

There was something horrible in the sudden rush of words, something horrible and unexpected. It made me feel sick, even though I knew. Maxim had gone very white. Favell looked at her foolishly, as though he had not understood. There was no sound but that of the falling rain. Then Colonel Julyan spoke, quietly, slowly.

'Mrs Danvers, can you think of any reason at all why Mrs de Winter would have taken her own life?'

'No,' she said, shaking her head. 'No.'

'There, you see?' said Favell quickly. 'It's impossible. She knows that as well as I do.'

'Be quiet, will you? Give Mrs Danvers time to think. She wrote that note some time during those hours she spent in London. There was something she wanted to tell you. Let Mrs Danvers read the note.'

She read it twice, shaking her head. 'It's no use,' she said. 'I don't know what she meant. If there was something important she had to tell Mr Jack she would have told me first.'

'Does anybody know how she spent that day in London?'

Favell swore under his breath. 'Look here, she left that note at my flat at three in the afternoon. The servant saw her. She must have driven down here straight after that.

'Mrs de Winter had an appointment to have her hair done,' said Mrs Danvers. 'I remember that, because I telephoned to London for her. Twelve until 1.30. She had lunch at her club after that.'

'Say it took her half an hour to have lunch; what was she doing from two o'clock until three?'

'Oh, who cares what she was doing?' shouted Favell. 'She didn't kill herself – that's the only thing that matters.'

'I have her appointment book locked away in my room,' said Mrs Danvers slowly. 'She may have noted down her appointments for that day. She was very careful in that way. She used to write everything down, and then mark it with a cross when it was done.'

'Well, de Winter; what do you say? Do you mind us seeing this book?'

'Of course not,' said Maxim. 'Why on earth should I?' Once again I saw Colonel Julyan give him that strange, quick look.

Mrs Danvers came back with a small red book. 'I was right,' she said. 'She had marked down her appointments, as I said.'

She gave the little book to Colonel Julyan. There was a long pause while he looked down the page. There was something about that moment that frightened me more than anything that had happened that evening. I could not look at Maxim.

'Ah!' he said. His finger was in the middle of the page. Something is going to happen, I thought; something terrible. 'Yes, here it is. "Hair at twelve", as Mrs Danvers said. And a cross beside it. She kept her appointment, then. "Lunch at the club", and a cross beside that. What have we here, though? "Baker, two o'clock." Who was Baker?' He looked at Maxim. Maxim shook his head. Then at Mrs Danvers. 'Baker?' repeated Mrs Danvers. 'She knew no one called Baker. I've never heard the name before.'

'Well, here it is!' said Colonel Julyan, giving her the little book. ' "Baker." And she's put a great cross beside it as though she wanted to break the pencil. It looks as though she saw this Baker, whoever he may have been. I believe if we knew who he was we would get to the bottom of the whole affair. She had no enemy, no one who had ever threatened her, no one she was afraid of?'

'Mrs de Winter afraid? She was afraid of nothing and no one. Only one thing ever worried her, and that was the idea of getting old, of illness, of dying in her bed. She said to me many times, "When I go, Danny, I want to go out quickly – like a light." That's the only thing that comforted me. They say drowning's painless, don't they?' Then suddenly she gave a cry, 'There's something here – right at the back, among the telephone numbers. "Baker: 0488." That's all.'

'That's his number all right,' said Colonel Julyan. 'But why didn't she put the exchange?'

'Try every telephone exchange in London!' said Favell. 'It will only take you all night, and Max wants to play for time, don't you, Max? And so should I, if I were in your shoes!'

'Could this mark beside the number possibly be an M?'

Mrs Danvers took the little book in her hands again. 'It might be. It's not like her usual M, but she may have written it in a hurry. Yes, it might be M.'

'Well?' said Maxim. 'Something had better be done about it. Frank! Go through and ask the exchange for Mayfair 0488.'

I stood quite still. Maxim did not look at me. Frank went into the little room. In a moment we heard him say: 'Is that Mayfair 0488? Can you tell me if anyone of the name of Baker lives there? Oh, I see. I'm so sorry. Yes, I must have got the wrong number. Thank you.'

Then he came back into the room. 'Someone called Lady Eastleigh lives at Mayfair 0488. They have never heard of Baker.'

Favell gave great shouts of laughter. 'Go on! What's the next exchange on the list?'

'Try Museum,' said Mrs Danvers.

Frank looked at Maxim. 'Go ahead,' said Maxim.

Again Frank went to the other room. He left the door wide open. 'Hullo – is that Museum 0488? Can you tell me if anyone of the name of Baker lives there? Oh – who is that speaking? Oh, yes. Yes, I understand. Can you give me the address? Yes; it's rather important.' He paused, and said to us over his shoulder, 'I think we've got him.'

Oh, don't let it be true! Don't let Baker be found! I knew who Baker was. I had known all along. I watched Frank lean forward suddenly, reaching for a pencil and paper. 'Hullo? Yes. I'm still here. Could you spell it? Thank you very much. Good night.' He came back into the room, the piece of paper in his hand. Frank, who loved Maxim, who did not know that with that one piece of paper he could destroy Maxim as well and truly as if he had a knife in his hand.

'It was the servant at an address in Bloomsbury. No one lives there. It is used during the day by a doctor. It seems that Baker has retired, and left the place six months ago. But we can find him all right. The man told me his address. I wrote it down on this piece of paper.'

It was then that Maxim looked at me for the first time that evening. And in his eyes I read a last message, a final goodbye. Favell, Mrs Danvers, Colonel Julyan, Frank with the slip of paper in his hand, they were all forgotten at this moment. Then he turned away and said to Frank: 'Well done. What's the address?'

'Somewhere near Barnet, to the north of London. But it's not on the telephone. We can't ring him up.'

'Can you throw any light on the matter now?' Colonel Julyan asked Mrs Danvers.

She shook her head. 'Mrs de Winter never needed a doctor. And like many strong people she hated them. We only had Dr Phillips from Kerrith here once. I've never heard her speak of this Dr Baker.'

'What the devil does it matter who he was? If it was of any importance, Danny would know. Rebecca had no secrets from her.'

'The servant at Museum 0488 told me that he was a very well-known doctor – a women's specialist.'

'H'm,' said Colonel Julyan. 'There must have been something wrong with her after all, but it seems very strange that she didn't say anything even to you, Mrs Danvers.'

'She was too thin,' said Favell. 'I told her so, but she only laughed. She said it suited her. Did it on purpose, I suppose, like all these women. She probably went to Baker for advice about what she should eat.'

'I can't understand it,' said Mrs Danvers. 'Dr Baker. Why didn't she tell me? She used to tell me everything.'

'Perhaps she didn't want to worry you,' said Colonel Julyan. 'She made an appointment with him, and saw him, and was going to tell you all about it that night.'

'And the note to Mr Jack,' said Mrs Danvers suddenly. '"I have something to tell you. I must see you"; she was going to tell him too.'

'I believe you're right after all,' said Favell. 'The note and the appointment do seem to go together. But what the devil was it all about? That's what I want to know. What was the matter with her?'

The truth shouted in their ears and they did not understand. I dared not look at them. I dared not even move.

'It ought to be quite easy to find out,' said Frank. 'I can write and ask him if he remembers an appointment last year with Mrs de Winter.'

'I don't know if he would answer you,' said Colonel Julyan. 'You know what these doctors are. The only way to get anything out of him would be to get de Winter to see him himself and explain things.'

'I'm ready to do whatever you suggest,' said Maxim quietly.

'Anything for time, eh?' said Favell. 'A lot can be done in twenty-four hours, can't it? Trains can be caught, ships can sail, planes can fly.'

I saw Mrs Danvers look sharply from Favell to Maxim, and I realized then that she had not known about Favell's accusation. At last she was beginning to understand. I could tell from the expression on her face. It's too late, I thought, she can't do anything to us now. She can't hurt us any more. Maxim was talking to Colonel Julyan.

'What do you suggest?' he said. 'Shall I drive to this address in the morning?'

'He's not going alone,' said Favell with a short laugh. 'I have a right to say that, haven't I? Send him up with Inspector Welch and I shan't object.'

If only Mrs Danvers would take her eyes away from Maxim. Frank had seen her now. He was watching her, confused and anxious. I saw him look once more at the piece of paper in his hand, on which he had written Dr Baker's address. Then he too looked at Maxim. I believe that he began to get some faint idea of the truth, because he went very white and put the paper down on the table.

'I don't think there is any need to bring Inspector Welch into the affair – yet,' said Colonel Julyan. His voice was different – harder. I did not like the way he used the word 'yet'. Why must he use it at all? I did not like it. 'If I go with de Winter, and stay with him the whole time, and bring him back, will that satisfy you?'

Favell looked at Maxim, then at Colonel Julyan. 'Yes,' he said slowly, 'yes, I suppose so. But for safety, do you mind if I come too?'

'No. Unfortunately, I think you have the right to ask that.'

'I rather think this Dr Baker is going to prove my case after all,' said Favell. He looked round at each one of us and began to laugh. I think he too had understood at last the meaning of that visit to the doctor.

'Well,' he said, 'what time are we going to start?'

'Nine o'clock?' said Colonel Julyan.

'Nine o'clock,' said Maxim.

'How do we know he won't run off in the night?' asked Favell. 'He's only got to slip round to the garage and get into his car.'

'Is my word good enough for you?' said Maxim, turning to Colonel Julyan. And for the first time Colonel Julyan paused. Maxim's face went pale. 'Mrs Danvers,' he said slowly, 'when Mrs de Winter and I go to bed tonight will you come up yourself and lock the door on the outside? And call us yourself, at seven in the morning?'

'Yes, sir,' said Mrs Danvers.

'Very well, then,' said Colonel Julyan shortly. 'I don't think there is anything else we need to discuss tonight. I shall be here at nine in the morning. You will have room for me in your car, de Winter?'

'Yes,' said Maxim.

'And Favell will follow us in his?'

'Right on your tail, my dear Colonel, right on your tail.'

Colonel Julyan came up to me and took my hand. 'Good night,' he said. 'You know how I feel for you in all this; there's no need for me to tell you. Get your husband to bed early if you can. It's going to be a long day.' He held my hand a minute, and then he turned away. It was strange the way he avoided my eye.

'I suppose I'm not going to be asked to dinner?' Favell said. 'Never mind, I'm looking forward to tomorrow. Goodbye then, old man. Pleasant dreams. Make the most of your night behind that locked door.' He turned and laughed at me, and then he went out of the room. Mrs Danvers followed him. Maxim and I were alone.

I held out my arms to him and he came to me like a child. I put my arms round him and held him. We did not say anything for a long time.

'We can sit together,' he said, at last, 'driving up in the car.'

'Yes.'

'Julyan won't mind.'

'No.'

'We shall have tomorrow night, too,' he said. 'They won't do anything immediately. Not for twenty-four hours perhaps.'

◆

I remember every detail of that evening. The curtains had been closed. It seemed strange to be sitting in the dining room and not looking out onto the gardens. It was like the beginning of autumn.

Later, the telephone rang. I heard Beatrice at the other end. 'Is that you? We've been trying to get you. We saw the evening papers,' she said. 'The result of the inquiry was a terrible shock to both Giles and myself. What does Maxim say about it?'

'I think it was a shock to everybody,' I said.

'But, my dear, I can't believe it. Why on earth would Rebecca have killed herself? The most unlikely person in the world! There must be a mistake somewhere.'

'I don't know.'

'What does Maxim say? Where is he?'

'People have been here,' I said. 'Colonel Julyan and others. Maxim is very tired. We're going up to London tomorrow.'

'What on earth for?'

'Something to do with the result. I can't really explain.'

'You ought to get it changed. Surely Colonel Julyan can do something? What are Justices of the Peace for? Old Horridge must have been mad. Why was she supposed to have done it? Someone ought to get hold of Tabb. How can he tell whether

87

those holes in the boat were made on purpose or not? Giles says of course it must have been the rocks.'

'They seemed to think not,' I said.

'If only I could have been there! No one seems to have made any effort. Is Maxim very upset?'

'He's tired. More tired than anything else.'

'Tell him he must try to get the result of the inquiry changed. It's so bad for the family. I'm telling everybody here that it's a mistake. Rebecca would never have killed herself. She wasn't the type.'

'It's no use,' I said. 'It's too late. Please, Beatrice, don't try to do anything. It will only make things worse. Please, Beatrice, just leave it alone.'

Thank God she had not been with us today! There was a sudden noise on the telephone line. I heard Beatrice saying, 'Hullo! Hullo!' and then there was silence. I went back to the library. In a few minutes the telephone began ringing again; I let it ring. I went and sat down at Maxim's feet. It went on ringing. I did not move. Maxim put his arms around me, and we kissed feverishly, desperately, like lovers who have not kissed before.

Chapter 10 The Visit to Dr Baker

When I awoke the next morning, just after six o'clock, and got up and went to the window, the grass was wet and the trees were hidden in a white mist; the air was cold, with the smell of autumn. As I knelt by the window looking down on to the rose garden, the events of the day before seemed far away and quite unreal. Here at Manderley a new day was starting; the creatures in the garden were not concerned with our troubles. A blackbird ran across the rose garden in quick, short rushes. A seabird hung in the air, silent and alone, and then spread his wings wide and floated down over the woods towards the Happy Valley. These things continued; our worries and fears did not change them. No one would ever hurt Manderley. It would lie always in its hollow, guarded by the woods, safe and secret, while the sea broke and ran and came again over the white stones of the little bay below.

My case looked unfamiliar as I dragged it out of a cupboard. It seemed so long since I had used it, yet it was only four months ago. In one of the pockets was a ticket for a theatre in Monte Carlo. It might have belonged to another age, another world. My bedroom began to take on the appearance of every room when the owner goes away – empty, unloved. When I was halfway down the passage I had a strange feeling that I must go back and look once more. I stood for a moment, looking at the open cupboard, the empty bed, the tea on the table. I wondered why they had the power to touch me, to sadden me, as though they were children who did not want me to go away.

After breakfast, Frank arrived. 'Colonel Julyan is waiting down at the gates,' he said. 'I'll be in the office all day, in case you telephone. After you've seen Baker you may find you want me, up in London.'

'Yes,' said Maxim. 'Yes, perhaps.'

'It's just nine now. You're on time. It's going to be sunny. You should have a good run.'

'We'd better be off,' said Maxim. 'Old Julyan will be getting worried.'

I climbed into the car beside Maxim. Frank shut the door.

'You will telephone, won't you?' he said.

'Yes, of course,' said Maxim.

I looked back at the house. Frith was standing at the top of the steps, and Robert just behind. My eyes filled with tears for no reason. I turned away, so that nobody would see. Then Maxim started up the car, and we turned the corner and the house was hidden from us.

We stopped at the gates and picked up Colonel Julyan. He looked doubtful when he saw me.

'It's going to be a long day,' he said. 'I don't think you should have attempted it. I would have taken care of your husband, you know.'

'I wanted to come,' I said.

He did not say any more about it, but got in the back. 'That man Favell said he would pick us up at the crossroads. If he's not there, don't wait; we would do much better without him.'

But when we came to the crossroads I saw the long green body of his car, and my heart sank. I had thought he might not be on time. He was sitting smoking at the wheel, hatless; he waved us on when he saw us. I settled down in my seat for the journey ahead, one hand on Maxim's knee.

The green car kept close behind us. We came to the edge of London at about three o'clock. It was then that I began to feel tired; the noise and the heat gave me a headache. It was hot. The streets had that dusty look of August, and the leaves hung still on the dull trees. There had been no rain here. There were too many people, too much noise. The drive through London seemed endless. By the time we were through it and out beyond Hampstead there was a sound in my head like the beating of a drum, and my eyes were burning. I wondered how tired Maxim was. He was pale, and there were shadows under his eyes.

When we came to Barnet itself, Colonel Julyan made him stop every few minutes. 'Can you tell us where a house called Roselands is? It belongs to a Dr Baker, who has retired and come to live here recently.' Behind us came Favell, his low green car covered with dust. It was a postman who pointed out the house in the end. A square house, with no name on the gate, which we had already passed twice. Maxim stopped the car at the side of the road. We sat silently for a few moments.

'Well, here we are,' said Colonel Julyan, 'and it's exactly twelve minutes past five. We shall catch them in the middle of their tea.'

We got out of the car, and Favell came up. We walked up the drive to the front door, a strange little party. Colonel Julyan rang the bell. A very young servant opened the door, and looked surprised that there were so many of us.

'Dr Baker?' said Colonel Julyan.

'Yes, sir; will you come in?'

She opened a door on the left, into a room which looked not much used in summer. Favell examined a picture on the wall. Colonel Julyan stood by the empty fireplace. Maxim and I looked out of the window.

Then the door opened and a man came into the room. He was of average height, rather long in the face, with a firm jaw. His hair was turning grey.

'Forgive me for keeping you waiting,' he said, looking a little surprised, as the servant had done, at seeing so many of us. 'I had to run upstairs and wash. I was in the garden when the bell rang. Won't you sit down?'

I sat down in the nearest chair, and waited.

'I'm so sorry to disturb you like this,' said Colonel Julyan. 'My name is Julyan. This is Mr de Winter – Mrs de Winter – Mr Favell. You may have seen Mr de Winter's name in the papers recently.'

'Oh?' said Dr Baker. 'Yes, yes – I suppose I have. Some inquiry or other, wasn't there? My wife was reading all about it.'

'It was said at the inquiry that the first Mrs de Winter killed herself,' said Favell, 'which I say is completely out of the question. Mrs de Winter was my cousin. I knew her very well. She would never have done such a thing. She had no reason to. What we want to know is, what the devil she came to see you about on the day she died?'

'You had better leave this to Julyan and myself,' Maxim said quietly. 'Dr Baker has not the faintest idea what you mean.' He turned to the doctor. 'We have driven up to see you today because we found your name and the telephone number of your old rooms in my first wife's appointment book. She seems to have been to see you at two o'clock on the last day she ever spent in London. Could you possibly check this for us?'

When Maxim had finished, Dr Baker shook his head. 'I'm very sorry,' he said, 'but I think you have made a mistake. I should have remembered the name de Winter. I've never attended a Mrs de Winter in my life.'

Colonel Julyan brought out the little book. 'Here it is, written down,' he said. '"Baker, two o'clock." And a big cross beside it, to show that the appointment was kept. And here is what looks like your number. "Museum 0488."'

Dr Baker examined it. 'That's very strange. Yes, the number is correct, as you say.'

'Could she have come to see you, and given another name?'

'Why, yes, that's possible. It's unusual, of course. I've never encouraged that sort of thing: it doesn't do us any good in the profession.'

'Would you have any record of the visit among your papers?' said Colonel Julyan. 'I know this is not normally done, but we do feel that her appointment with you must be connected with her—'

'—murder,' said Favell, interrupting him.

Dr Baker opened his eyes wide. 'I had no idea there was any question of that,' he said quietly. 'Of course I'll do anything in my power to help you. If you'll excuse me for a few minutes I will go and look among my papers. There should be a record of every appointment, and a description of the case.' He went out.

'Seems a good sort,' said Colonel Julyan.

'Why didn't he offer us a drink?' said Favell. 'Keeps it locked up, I suppose. I don't think much of him. I don't believe he's going to help us after all.'

Dr Baker came back into the room with books and a pile of papers in his hands. He carried them over to the table. 'I've brought the collection for the last year,' he said. 'I haven't been through them since we moved. I only retired six months ago, you know.' He opened a book and began turning the pages. I watched him helplessly. He would find it, of course. It was only a question of minutes now, of seconds. 'The seventh, eighth, tenth,' he said. 'The twelfth, did you say? At two o'clock? Ah!'

We none of us moved. We all watched his face.

'I saw a Mrs Danvers on the twelfth at two o'clock.'

'Danny? What on earth—' began Favell, but Maxim cut him short.

'She gave a false name, of course,' he said. 'That was obvious from the first. Do you remember the visit now, Dr Baker?'

But Dr Baker was already searching in his papers. He soon found the notes, and read them rapidly. 'Yes,' he said. 'Mrs Danvers; I remember now.' He put the papers down. 'Of course,' he said to Maxim, 'you realize that this is very unprofessional? But your wife is dead, and I quite understand that the situation is unusual. You want to know if I can suggest any reason why your wife might have taken her life? I think I can. The woman who called herself Mrs Danvers was very seriously ill.'

He paused. He looked at every one of us in turn.

'I remember her perfectly well. She came to me a week before the date you mentioned, and I took some X-ray photographs of her. This second visit was to hear what the X-rays showed. I remember her holding out her hand for them. "I want to know the truth," she said. "I don't want you to be gentle with me. Just tell me." '

He paused and looked down at the notes. I waited. Why couldn't he finish with it and let us go? Why must we sit there, waiting, our eyes on his face?

'Well, she asked for the truth, and I let her have it. Some

people are better for it; hiding the facts does them no good. She stood it very well. She said she had guessed it for some time. Then she paid me and went out. I never saw her again.'

He closed the book and put the papers back in the pile.

'The pain was still slight, but the growth was deep-rooted. In three or four months' time there would have been nothing to do but try to kill the pain, and wait. There is nothing else anyone can do in a case like that.'

No one said a word.

'Of course she still *looked* a perfectly healthy woman. Rather too thin, I remember, and rather pale; but then that's the fashion now. The X-rays showed a certain faulty development in some of the organs, I remember, which meant she could never have had a child, but that was nothing to do with the disease.'

I remember hearing Colonel Julyan speak, saying something about Dr Baker being very kind to have taken so much trouble. 'You have told us all we want to know,' he said, 'and if we could possibly have a copy of your notes, it might be very useful.'

'Of course, of course.'

'We may not need it at all. But either de Winter or I will write. Here is my card.'

'I'm so glad to have been of use. It never entered my head that Mrs de Winter and Mrs Danvers could be the same person.'

'No; naturally.'

'You'll be returning to London, I imagine? Your best way is to turn sharp left at the corner, then right by the church. After that it's a straight road.'

'Thank you. Thank you very much.'

We came out onto the drive, and walked to the car. No one spoke. Favell looked grey and shaken. 'I never had the slightest idea,' he said. 'She kept it a secret from everyone, even Danny. What a terrible thing, eh? Not the sort of thing one would ever connect with Rebecca. Do you people feel like a drink? This business has really shocked me, and I don't mind admitting it. My God!' He leaned up against the car, and shaded his eyes with his hand.

'Pull yourself together, man,' said Colonel Julyan.

'Oh, you're all right! You're fine!' said Favell, standing up straight and looking at Colonel Julyan and Maxim. 'Baker will supply what you want in black and white, free of cost, whenever you send the word.'

'Shall we get into the car and go?' said Colonel Julyan. 'We can make our plans as we drive.'

We got in, but Favell still leaned against the car.

'I should advise you to get straight back to your flat and go to bed,' said Colonel Julyan, 'and drive slowly. I may as well warn you now that as a Justice of the Peace I have certain powers that will prove effective if you are ever seen in the Kerrith area again. We know how to deal with people like you, strange though it may seem.'

Favell was watching Maxim. He had lost the grey colour now, and the old unpleasant smile was forming on his lips. 'Yes, it's been a stroke of luck for you, Max, hasn't it?' he said slowly. 'You think you've won, don't you? But the law can still get you, and so can I, in a different way . . .'

Maxim started the engine. 'Have you anything else to say?' he said. 'Because if so you had better say it now.'

'No,' said Favell. 'No. I won't keep you. You can go.' He stepped back, with the smile still on his lips. The car slid forward. As we turned the corner I looked back and saw him standing there, watching us; as he waved his hand, he was laughing.

We drove on for a while in silence. Then Colonel Julyan spoke. 'He can't do anything,' he said. 'That smile and that wave were only part of his pretence. They are all alike, his sort. He hasn't a thread of a case to bring now. Baker would wreck it. I always felt the solution was connected with Baker. The way she never even

95

told Mrs Danvers. She knew something was wrong. Terrible! Enough to send a young and lovely woman right off her head. I suppose you never had any idea of this?'

'No,' said Maxim. 'No.'

'Of course some people always live in fear of a disease like that. Women especially. That must have been the case with your wife. She had enough courage for everything except that. She could not face pain. Well, she was spared that, at any rate.'

'Yes,' said Maxim.

'I don't think it would do any harm if I quietly let it be known down in Kerrith that a London doctor has suggested an explanation. In case people talk. You never can tell, you know. People are funny. If they knew about Mrs de Winter it might make it a lot easier for you. I don't suppose the newspapermen will worry you any more, that's one good thing. You'll find they'll drop the whole affair in a day or two.' We drove on southwards, and entered London once more. 'Half past six. What are you going to do? I've got a sister living in St John's Wood, and I think I'll ask her to give me dinner, then catch the last train down. I'm sure she would be happy to see you both as well.'

Maxim paused, and looked at me. 'It's very kind of you,' he said, 'but I think not. I must ring up Frank, and one thing and another. I think we'll have a quiet meal somewhere, and start off again afterwards. We'll spend the night at a hotel on the way down.'

'Of course,' said Colonel Julyan. 'I quite understand.'

When we came to his sister's house, Maxim said: 'It's impossible to thank you for all you've done today. You know what I feel.'

'My dear man, I've been only too glad. You must put the whole thing behind you now. I'm pretty sure you won't have any more trouble from Favell. If you do, I shall know how to deal with him.' He got out of the car, collecting his coat and his map. 'I should get away for a bit. Take a short holiday. Go abroad, perhaps.' He cleared his throat. 'It is just possible that certain little difficulties might come up. From one or two people in the area. One never knows what Tabb has been saying, and so on. You know the old saying? "Out of sight, out of mind." If people are not there to be talked about, the talk dies. It's the way of the world.'

He stood for a moment, counting his things. 'I've got everything, I think; coat, cap, stick, map, all complete. Well, goodbye, both of you. Don't get overtired. It's been a long day.' He turned in at the gate and walked up the steps.

We drove away down the road and turned the corner. I leaned back in my seat and closed my eyes. Now that we were alone again and the anxiety was over, the feeling was one of almost unbearable relief. When Maxim stopped, I opened my eyes. We were opposite a little restaurant in a narrow street in Soho.

'You're tired. Empty and tired and fit for nothing. You'll be better when you've had something to eat. So shall I. We'll go in here and order dinner right away. I can telephone Frank too.'

We got out of the car. There was no one in the restaurant. It was dark and cool. We went to a table in the corner. 'Favell was right about wanting a drink,' said Maxim. 'I want one too, and so do you.'

My drink was soft, warming, strangely comforting.

'When we've had dinner we'll drive very slowly and quietly. It will be cool, too, in the evening. We'll find somewhere on the road to stay the night; then we can go on to Manderley in the morning.'

'Yes,' I said.

Maxim's eyes looked large, and they were ringed with shadows. They looked very dark against his white face.

'How much of the truth do you think Julyan guessed?'

I watched him over my glass, but said nothing.

'He knew,' said Maxim slowly, 'of course he knew.'

'If he did, he'll never say anything.'

'No,' said Maxim.

He ordered another drink. We sat silent and peaceful in our dark corner.

'I believe that Rebecca lied to me on purpose. She wanted me to kill her. She planned the whole thing. That's why she laughed. That's why she stood there laughing when she died.'

I went on with my drink. It was all over. All settled. It did not matter any more. There was no need for Maxim to look white and troubled.

'It was her last joke – the best of them all. And I'm not sure she hasn't won, even now.'

'What do you mean? How can she have won?'

'I don't know,' he said. 'I don't know.' He finished his second drink, then got up. 'I'm going to telephone Frank,' he said.

I sat there in my corner; and soon the waiter brought me my fish. It was hot, and very good. I had another drink, too. I smiled at the waiter, and asked for some more bread in French, for no reason. It was quiet and friendly in the restaurant. Maxim and I were together; everything was over.

Soon Maxim came back again. 'Well,' I said, 'how was Frank?'

'Frank was all right. Something rather strange, though,' Maxim said slowly. 'He thinks that Mrs Danvers has gone. It seems she had been packing up all day, and a man from the station came for her things. Frith told Frank about it, and Frank told Frith to ask Mrs Danvers to come to see him at the office. He waited but she never came. About ten minutes before I rang up, Frith telephoned Frank again and said that there had been a long-distance telephone call for Mrs Danvers at about ten past six. Soon after that, he found her room empty. She must have gone straight out of the house and through the woods. She never went past the gates.'

'Isn't it a good thing?' I said. 'It saves us a lot of trouble. We would have had to send her away, in any case. I believe she guessed, too. There was a look on her face, that night. I kept thinking of it, coming up in the car.'

'I don't like it,' said Maxim. 'I don't like it.'

'She can't do anything. It was Favell who telephoned, of course. He must have told her about Baker. He would tell her what Colonel Julyan said about threatening us. They won't dare to do it.'

'I'm not thinking of that.'

'What else can they do? We've got to do as Colonel Julyan said – we've got to forget it. It's all over, dear; it's finished. Your fish will get cold. Eat it – it will do you good. You need something inside you. You're tired.' I was using the words he had used to me. I felt better and stronger. It was I now who was taking care of him. Things were going to be different in the future. With Mrs Danvers gone, I would learn how to run the house. People would come to stay, and I would not mind. There would be the interest of seeing to their rooms, arranging flowers and books, ordering the food. We would have children. Surely we would have children.

'Have you finished?' said Maxim suddenly. 'I don't think I want any more. Only coffee. Black, very strong, please – and the bill,' he added to the waiter.

I wondered why we must go so soon. It was comfortable in the restaurant, and there was nothing to take us away. I liked sitting there, with my head against the back of the chair, planning the future in a lazy, pleasant way. I could have gone on sitting there for a long while.

'Listen,' said Maxim, 'do you think you could sleep in the car if I wrapped you up and put you in the back? There's a cushion there, and my coat as well. I have a feeling I must get down tonight. We'll be there by half past two.'

'You'll be terribly tired.'

'No.' He shook his head. 'I shall be all right. I want to get home. Something's wrong. I know it is.' His face was anxious, strange, as he began arranging things in the back of the car.

'What *can* be wrong?' I said. 'It seems so strange to worry now, when everything's over. I can't understand you.'

He did not answer. He covered me with his coat. It was very comfortable. Much better than I imagined. I settled the cushion under my head.

'Are you all right? Are you sure you don't mind?'

'No,' I said, smiling. 'I'm all right. Much better to do this and get home. We'll be at Manderley long before sunrise.'

He got in, and we started on our journey. I shut my eyes. The car moved smoothly. A hundred pictures came to my mind, mixed together in a senseless pattern. Ben smiling foolishly; Mrs Danvers standing at the top of the stairs in her black dress; the postman who had pointed out the house to us today; Jasper chasing across the grass. I fell into a strange, broken sleep, waking now and then to the reality of my bed in the car and the sight of Maxim's back in front of me. There were the lights of passing cars on the road; there were villages with lights behind closed curtains. At last I sat up, and pushed the hair away from my face.

'I can't sleep,' I said. 'It's no use.'

'You've been sleeping,' said Maxim. 'You've slept for hours. It's quarter past two. We'll soon be in Kerrith.'

It was cold. I was trembling in the darkness of the car. 'I'll come beside you,' I said. 'We'll be at Manderley by three.'

I climbed over and sat beside him. I put my hand on his knee.

'You're cold,' he said.

'Yes.'

The hills rose in front of us, disappeared, and rose again. It was quite dark. The stars had gone.

'What time did you say it was?' I asked.

'Twenty past two.'

'It's funny – it looks almost as though day were breaking over there, beyond those hills. It can't be, though; it's too early.'

'It's the wrong direction. You're looking west.'

'I know,' I said. 'It's funny, isn't it?'

He did not answer, and I went on watching the sky. It seemed to get lighter even as I looked. Like the first red light of sunrise. Little by little, it spread across the sky.

'It's in the winter you see the northern lights, isn't it?' I said. 'Not in the summer?'

'That's not the northern lights,' he said. 'That's Manderley.'

I looked at him and saw his face. I saw his eyes.

'Maxim!' I said. 'What is it?'

He drove much faster. We came to the top of the hill: there to the left of us was the silver thread of the river, widening towards its mouth at Kerrith, ten kilometres away. The road to Manderley lay ahead. There was no moon. The sky above our heads was inky black. But the sky on the horizon was not black at all. It was red, like blood. And the ashes blew towards us with the salt wind from the sea.

ACTIVITIES

Chapters 1–2

Before you read

1 Read the Introduction to this book and answer these questions about the story.
   a What is Manderley?
   b Where is it?
   c Who owns it?
   d Who is his housekeeper?
   e Who was his first wife?
   f Who is his second wife?
   g When is the story set?

2 Rebecca is already dead before this story begins, so why do you think the novel is called *Rebecca*?

3 Look at the Word list at the back of the book. Complete these paragraphs with words from the list.
   a The house was at the end of a long .... , on the top of a .... , above a sandy .... During the day there were people on the beach, but at night it was .... Nothing .... us – not even the sound of the waves.
   b When I first gave a speech, I felt .... and nervous. My voice shook and my hands .... I was .... to succeed, though, so I tried not to show my .... It was a great .... when I finally finished the speech and could sit down.

4 These people will all be important in the story. What are the professional responsibilities of people like these? Which do you think the most difficult job is? Why?
   a companion   a business manager   a colonel
   a police inspector   a harbour master

While you read

5 Read the first two pages of the story. Match the time expressions with the right sentences.

   a The storyteller dreams of Manderley.   now

   b Manderley does not exist any more.   some time ago

   c She works for Mrs Van Hopper and   last night
      hasn't been to Manderley.

6 Are these sentences right (✓) or wrong (✗)?

   a Maxim de Winter's wife died of a terrible illness.   .....

   b Mrs Van Hopper's nephew has been to Manderley.   .....

   c Mr de Winter enjoys his conversation with Mrs
      Van Hopper.   .....

   d The storyteller feels awkward when she has her
      first meal alone with Mr de Winter.   .....

   e Everyone at Manderley makes Mrs de Winter feel
      at home.   .....

   f The first Mrs de Winter had a bedroom with a sea view.   .....

After you read

7 Answer the questions.

   a Is Maxim de Winter well known among people of his social class?

   b Was the storyteller born into a rich family?

   c Who enjoys talking about other people?

   d Why are Mr and Mrs de Winter going to use the east wing?

   e Has Mr de Winter always lived at Manderley?

   f Who runs the house at Manderley?

8 What feelings do Mrs de Winter and Mrs Danvers have for each other? Write the words in the boxes.

scorn   mistrust   fear   hatred   awkwardness

Mrs Danvers feels ...	Mrs de Winter feels...

9 Work with two other students. You are servants at Manderley. It is the end of Mrs de Winter's first day there. Discuss Mr de Winter's choice of wife. Do you approve?

10 Discuss these statements from the story. Do you agree with them? Why (not)?

   a Moonlight can play strange tricks with the imagination.
   b Dullness is better than fear.
   c The fever of first love ... is ... a misery too.

Chapters 3–4

Before you read

11 Discuss these questions.

   a Why do you think Maxim seems angry about his new wife's anxieties at the end of their first day at Manderley?
   b How do you think life will become more difficult for his wife in the next part of the story?

While you read

12 Who or what:

   a says what she thinks?   ....
   b occasionally gets very angry?   ....
   c is jealous of Mrs de Winter?   ....
   d is noisy and stupid?   ....
   e watches Mrs de Winter go into the
      cottage?   ....
   f wants to forget about the cottage?   ....

13 What does Mrs de Winter learn about Rebecca's death? Complete the paragraph.

   Rebecca's was washed .... when her .... turned over and sank. She .... as she was trying to swim to the shore. Her body was found .... months later, ... kilometres up the coast.

After you read

14 What information supports each of these statements?

    a Beatrice is a good friend to Mrs de Winter.

    b Maxim has returned to Manderley too soon.

    c Mrs Danvers will always be an enemy of Mrs de Winter.

    d Ben has mental problems.

    e Mrs de Winter has little confidence in herself.

    f Frank Crawley prefers Mrs de Winter to Rebecca.

15 Work with a partner. Re-read the argument between Maxim and his wife after their visit to the bay. Then close your books and act out the argument.

Chapters 5–6

Before you read

16 In these chapters, who do you think will say to Mrs de Winter:

    a 'I don't want to be put in the madhouse.'

    b 'Sometimes I wonder if she comes back to Manderley and watched you and Mr de Winter together.'

    c 'What the devil do you think you are doing?'

    d 'He thinks, you see, you did it on purpose.'

17 Discuss how the relationship between Maxim de Winter and his wife could get worse.

While you read

18 Circle the words that are wrong. Write the correct words.

    a Ben is afraid of going to the boathouse. ....

    b Favell is an old friend of Max. ....

    c Mrs de Winter visits the east wing. ....

    d Rebecca spent her last evening with Maxim. ....

    e Mrs de Winter dresses as the Queen of England for the fancy-dress party. ....

    f Maxim is delighted with her choice of clothes. ....

g Beatrice dressed in similar clothes at
a previous dance. ....

h Mrs de Winter was tricked into
wearing the clothes by Clarice. ....

After you read

19 Work with a partner. Act out a conversation after the fancy-dress
party between one of these pairs.

a Mrs de Winter and Maxim

b Mrs Danvers and Frith in the kitchen

c Beatrice and her husband on the way home

20 Imagine that you had been invited to the fancy-dress party at
Manderley. What would you have worn? Why? Tell the class.

21 Discuss everything that you now know about Rebecca. What kind
of person was she?

Chapter 7

Before you read

22 Discuss these questions.

a Mrs de Winter is beginning to feel that her marriage has failed.
Why? Is she right to believe that? Why (not)?

b In the next chapter, a sunken boat is found. What secrets might
the boat hold?

While you read

23 Complete these headlines from the local newspaper.

a SHIP RUNS ONTO ROCKS IN HEAVY ....

b .... FINDS MANDERLEY SAILING BOAT

c .... FOUND IN MANDERLEY BOAT

24 Are these statements right (✓) or wrong (✗)?

   a Rebecca died accidentally. ......

   b Rebecca and Max were happily married. ......

   c Rebecca was attractive and charming. ......

   d Manderley was less important to Max than
happiness. ......

   e Rebecca had other lovers. ......

   f She told Max she was going to have another
man's baby. ......

   g The sailing boat hit the rocks and sank. ......

   h Colonel Julyan is worried about the effect of
an inquiry on the de Winters. ......

   i He doesn't seem to be suspicious of Maxim. ......

   j The newspapers accuse Maxim of murder. ......

   k Only the de Winters know the truth about
Rebecca's death. ......

After you read

25 Discuss these questions.

   a Why is Mrs de Winter happy at the end of the chapter, although
she has learnt terrible things about her husband?

   b How would you feel, if you were her, about your marriage, your
husband, his first wife and his family home? What would you
do now?

Chapters 8–9

Before you read

26 Which of these people do you think will be at the public inquiry?
Why will they attend?

   Mr and Mrs de Winter   Frank   Mrs Danvers   Jack Favell   Ben
Mr Tabb, the boatbuilder   Beatrice and Giles   Dr Phillips

27 Which information presented at and after the inquiry is harmful to Maxim's case? Tick (✓) the damaging facts.

   a The boat was in good condition. .....
   b The wind wasn't strong enough to turn the boat over. .....
   c Rebecca was careless. .....
   d The boat didn't hit rocks. .....
   e There were three holes in the bottom of the boat. .....
   f Rebecca had sent a note to Favell. .....
   g Ben says he has never seen Favell. .....
   h Mrs Danvers says that Rebecca wouldn't have killed herself. .....
   i Rebecca had an appointment with a doctor on the day she died. .....

After you read

28 Answer the questions.
   a Why didn't Favell produce the note at the inquiry?
   b Why doesn't Colonel Julyan believe Favell at first?
   c Why does Maxim ask Mrs Danvers to lock their bedroom door from the outside?
   d How many people are going to London to see Dr Baker?

29 Work in group of three. You know that Maxim is guilty, but what do you think should happen to him? Come to an agreement and then tell the rest of the class your decision.
   Student A: You think that Maxim should be charged with murder and hanged. Explain why.
   Student B: You think that it is in nobody's interest to punish Maxim. Explain why.
   Student C: You think that Maxim must be punished, but not for murder. Explain why.

Chapter 10

Before you read

30 Discuss these questions. What do you think?

    a What will Colonel Julyan learn from Dr Baker?

    b How will this story end for these people?

        Maxim   Mrs de Winter   Mrs Danvers   Favell

While you read

31 Circle the right answers.

    a Mrs de Winter feels *happy / sad* when she leaves Manderley.

    b Rebecca booked her appointment in the name of *Mrs de Winter / Mrs Danvers*.

    c Rebecca was *dying / expecting a baby*.

    d Favell *knew / didn't know* the truth about Rebecca.

    e Colonel Julyan probably *believes / doesn't believe* that Rebecca killed herself.

    f Maxim thinks that Rebecca wanted to die *in her boat / by his hands*.

    g Mrs Danvers *is / isn't* at Manderley when the fire starts.

After you read

32 Who is talking? What are they talking about?

    a 'I think you've made a mistake. I should have remembered the name de Winter.'

    b 'I don't want you to be gentle with me. Just tell me.'

    c 'He can't do anything. That smile and that wave were only part of his pretence.'

    d 'You know the old saying? "Out of sight, out of mind."'

    e 'It was her last joke – the best of them all.'

    f 'Isn't it a good thing? It saves us a lot of trouble.'

    g 'It looks almost as though day were breaking over there, beyond those hills.'

33 Discuss what happened at Manderley on that last night. Who set fire to it and why?

34 Read the first two pages of the novel again.

    a Will the de Winters ever go home? Why (not)?

    b Are they happy now? Why (not)?

Writing

35 Imagine that you are a reporter for a local newspaper. Write one of the newspaper articles referred to on pages 58–9 for the front page of your paper. Make it as exciting as possible.

36 Imagine that you were standing on the cliffs above the cottage on the night that Maxim killed Rebecca. Write a statement for the police of everything you saw and heard.

37 Write a telephone conversation between Favell and Mrs Danvers after the visit to the doctor in London in the final chapter.

38 Choose a frightening scene from the novel and re-write it for the actors in a short film. Describe the setting and the characters and write the conversation in your own words. Describe where the characters stand and move to, the lighting and the music.

39 Compare Maxim's relationships with his first and second wives.

40 Imagine that Manderley was not burnt down. Maxim and his wife arrive at the house in the middle of the night and find Mrs Danvers waiting for them. Write the conversation between these characters.

41 A few months after Manderley burns down, Frank Crawley receives a letter from the owner of another large house. Mrs Danvers has asked for the job of housekeeper and the man would like Frank's opinion of her professional and personal qualities. Write his reply.

42 *Rebecca* takes place in England in the 1930s. Compare the de Winters' lifestyle then with your family's life today.

43 Explain how and why Mrs de Winter protects her husband. Would you behave in the same way, if you were in her position?

44 Explain how Daphne du Maurier makes the story exciting for her readers.

WORD LIST

alike (adj) similar to each other

anxiety (n) the feeling of being anxious

approve (v) to agree to something; to believe that someone or something is acceptable

ash (n) the soft grey powder that is left after something has been burned

at any rate a phrase used to state one good fact among other bad ones

awkward (adj) embarrassed and shy

bay (n) a part of a coastline where the land curves in

cliff (n) a high steep rock or piece of land, often next to the sea

colonel (n) an officer with a high position in the army

companion (n) someone who you spend a lot of time with

cottage (n) a small house in the country

deserted (adj) empty and quiet

determined (adj) wanting to do something very much, so you will not let anyone or anything stop you

disturb (v) to interrupt what someone is doing; if you feel **disturbed**, you are worried or nervous

fancy dress (n) clothes that you wear for fun or for a party and that make you look like a different person

horizon (n) the place where the land or sea seems to meet the sky

misery (n) a feeling of great unhappiness

modesty (n) the admirable quality of not talking proudly about your achievements or abilities

organ (n) a part of your body, for example your heart, that has a special purpose

rightful (adj) morally and legally correct

relief (n) the feeling that you have when you stop worrying about something

scorn (n/v) an opinion that someone or something is stupid or worthless

slope (n/v) a surface that is higher at one end than the other

somehow (adv) for a reason that you are not sure about; in a way, but you do not know how

stroke of luck (n) something lucky that happens to you

thread (n) something long and very thin, like a long piece of cotton

track (n) a narrow road or path with a rough surface

tremble (v) to shake because you are worried, afraid or excited

weed (n) a wild plant that grows where it is not wanted

X-ray (n) a photograph of the inside of your body, taken by a special machine

Heart of Darkness
Joseph Conrad

Resting one night on a boat on the River Thames, Charlie Marlow tells his friends about his experiences as a steamboat captain on the River Congo. There, in the heart of Africa, his search for the extraordinary Mr Kurtz caused him to question his own nature and values – and the nature and values of his society.

The Hound of the Baskervilles
Sir Arthur Conan Doyle

Sir Charles Baskerville is found dead just outside his home, Baskerville Hall. Many of the Baskerville family have died mysteriously. People say that they were killed by a gigantic devil-like creature – the Hound of the Baskervilles! Can that be true? And can Sherlock Holmes save the new owner of Baskerville Hall from a terrible death?

Sherlock Holmes Short Stories
Sir Arthur Conan Doyle

In these six stories we join the brilliant detective, Sherlock Holmes, and his friend Dr Watson, in a variety of exciting adventures. These include several suspicious deaths, the mystery of the engineer with the missing thumb, and the strange case of the two men who share a very unusual name.

There are hundreds of Penguin Readers to choose from – world classics, film adaptations, modern-day crime and adventure, short stories, biographies, American classics, non-fiction, plays ...

For a complete list of all Penguin Readers titles, please contact your local Pearson Longman office or visit our website.

Crime and Punishment
Fyodor Dostoevsky

Raskolnikoff, a young student, has been forced to give up his university studies because of lack of money. He withdraws from society and, poor and lonely, he develops a plan to murder a greedy old moneylender. Surely the murder of one worthless old woman would be excused, even approved of, if it made possible a thousand good deeds? But this crime is just the beginning of the story. Afterwards he must go on a journey of self-discovery. He must try to understand his motives and explain them to others. Can he succeed?

The Testament
John Grisham

Nate O'Riley is a powerful Washington lawyer. Returning to work after a long stay in hospital is difficult for Nate. Then he is sent on a journey that takes him from the tense courtrooms of Washington to the dangerous swamps of Brazil. It is a journey that will change his life forever . . .

The Talented Mr Ripley
Patricia Highsmith

Tom Ripley goes to Italy. He needs to find Dickie Greenleaf. Dickie's father wants him to go back to America. But Tom likes Italy, and he likes Dickie's money. Tom wants to stay in Italy, and he will do anything to get what he wants. *The Talented Mr Ripley is now an exciting movie with Matt Damon, Gwyneth Paltrow and Jude Law.*

There are hundreds of Penguin Readers to choose from – world classics, film adaptations, modern-day crime and adventure, short stories, biographies, American classics, non-fiction, plays ...

For a complete list of all Penguin Readers titles, please contact your local Pearson Longman office or visit our website.

www.penguinreaders.com

The Pelican Brief
John Grisham

In Washington, two Supreme Court judges are murdered and only the young and beautiful law student Darby Shaw knows why. She has uncovered a deadly secret but will anyone believe her? Can she stay alive long enough to persuade them she is right?

The Body
Stephen King

Gordie Lanchance and his three friends are always ready for adventure. When they hear about a dead body in the forest they go to look for it. Then they discover how cruel the world can be.

The Prisoner of Zenda
Anthony Hope

Rudolf Rassendyll is a daring young man, always looking for adventure. He visits Rurutania to see the crowning of the new king. The two men are surprised to find that they look exactly the same! But soon Rudolf is involved in a dangerous game of pretence – he plays the part of the king while the real king is held prisoner in the Castle of Zenda.

Longman Dictionaries

Express yourself with confidence!

*Longman has led the way in ELT dictionaries since 1935.
We constantly talk to students and teachers around the
world to find out what they need from a learner's dictionary.*

Why choose a Longman dictionary?

Easy to understand

Longman invented the Defining Vocabulary – 2000 of the most
common words which are used to write the definitions in our
dictionaries. So Longman definitions are always clear and easy
to understand.

Real, natural English

All Longman dictionaries contain natural examples taken from
real-life that help explain the meaning of a word and show you
how to use it in context.

Avoid common mistakes

Longman dictionaries are written specially for learners, and we
make sure that you get all the help you need to avoid common
mistakes. We analyse typical learners' mistakes and include
notes on how to avoid them.

Innovative CD-ROMs

Longman are leaders in dictionary CD-ROM innovation. Did
you know that a dictionary CD-ROM includes features to help
improve your pronunciation, help you practice for exams and
improve your writing skills?

**For details of all Longman dictionaries, and to choose
the one that's right for you, visit our website:**

www.longman.com/dictionaries